THE WALL BETWEEN THE WORLDS

Ruth Fox

The Bridges Trilogy
by Ruth Fox
available from Hague Publishing

The City of Silver Light
Across the Bridge of Ice
The Wall Between the Worlds

THE WALL BETWEEN THE WORLDS

© 2020 by Hague Publishing
Paperback Edition 2020
E-book Edition 2020

Hague Publishing
PO Box 451
Bassendean Western Australia 6934
Email: contact@haguepublishing.com
Web: www.haguepublishing.com

ISBN: 978-0-6485714-9-0

Cover Art: The Wall Between the Worlds by Ruth Fox

Typeset Century Schoolbook 12/14

Dedication

Wow. I began The Bridges Trilogy over a decade ago, with a half-formed idea and a kind-of impression of where I thought it would go. Now it's complete and I still can't believe it's done!

First and most importantly, I'd like to thank Hague Publishing. What a wonderful experience creating these books has been. Thank you for making the process enjoyable and for helping hone the world of Cassidy Heights and Shar.

Thank you to Mum and Dad for encouraging my writing, buying me notebooks when I was twelve, helping me to save for my first laptop when I was eighteen, and teaching me everything both creative and practical in life.

Thank you to Conan, my husband and partner in all things.

Thank you to my boys for the constant reminder of why I do what I do.

Last, but by no means least, thank you to my readers. I really can't express what it means to have shared these books with you.

Prologue

SHARNA looks nervous.

I'm wondering what she has to be nervous about – she's not the one facing the Beige Mile. I call it that in my head. It's not Green, and it's not as dull, or as dingy as the one in the prison in that Stephen King movie, but it's just as scary.

The phone beeps and she jumps. I wonder what's up. I mean, I've got to know her pretty well lately, with all the time I've been spending sitting outside the reception office, waiting to see Mrs Hildebrand. Sharna is a monitor, which means she helps out in the office during lunch times, filing and organising papers, and typing up papers, and putting papers in pigeonholes instead of sitting outside chatting about the latest magazine quiz like normal girls.

Sharna doesn't have a whole heap of friends and likes to keep to herself. She has a habit of talking over the top of other people. And she's got this whole thing about the environment. She knows everything there is to know about endangered pandas and she has stickers on her bag for WWF and Greenpeace.

I've never been a good student like her. But, somehow, lately I've been even worse than usual. I'm coming down here almost every day. Even so, it doesn't get any less scary, the more often you do it. The only good thing is that while I'm here, I'm not in Maths, or Science, or English, or any subject that involves books and teachers asking you questions. Books give me a headache, and not knowing the answers to questions just makes me feel stupid.

Sharna checks the phone – she's not allowed to answer calls from outside lines, but it must be one of the teachers in one of the staff rooms, because she picks it up.

'Yes, of course, I've got all of that right here,' she says into the phone. 'I'll pass it along to Mrs Hildebrand. Okay. Okay. Not at all.'

She drops the phone, tapping the finger of one hand on her desk while riffling through some papers with the other. 'I know Alice put it here somewhere . . .'

The door to Mrs Hildebrand's office opens and some kid comes out. He's wearing a brown jumper that doesn't fit properly and his long blond hair – not longish hair, like mine, but actually *down to his shoulders*, I'm not kidding – is tied back with an elastic. He's tall and thin and his skin is just-seen-a-ghost pale.

There's lots of new kids at school lately, since a couple of the high schools got damaged in this massive snowstorm a few weeks ago, and their students ended up coming here. But something about this guy is just . . . weird.

'Alice left me some forms for your guardian to sign, Aaron,' Sharna says, looking up. 'Just . . . ah, crap. Just a moment, okay? Everything's a mess . . .'

Aaron smiles politely.

'I . . . well, here's a pen. If you can write down your address, I'll post them to your . . . your guardian . . .'

Aaron takes the proffered pen, but she sucks in a little breath when his hand touches hers.

'They're in the drawer,' he says.

She looks up, puzzled.

'The papers,' he clarifies. 'You put them in the drawer.'

'Oh – I did, too.' She pulls out the correct papers and gives Aaron a bemused smile. 'How did –'

The phone bleeps again, and she picks it up, giving me a chance to survey this newest new kid. I wonder if he's Swedish or Icelandic or something. He speaks strangely, like he's been taught English by a Professor of Language or something – every word precise and properly formed.

He turns and I don't look away quickly enough. He sees me watching him.

His eyes. They're really, really blue. They're *creepy*. No one has eyes like that.

'Mikhal?' Sharna says, breaking into the

moment as she puts the phone down, still not looking at me. 'That was Mrs Hildebrand. She's ready to see you now.'

I gulp.

She looks up at me. 'Hey, Mikhal, thanks for inviting me to your party the other week.'

'Did you have fun? You danced with Jake, right?'

She smiles. 'Oh. Yeah, it was good to go out for once . . . anyway.' She nods towards Mrs Hildebrand's door. 'It's okay. She's in a good mood today.'

I laugh. It comes out short and sharp. I know she's just trying to make me feel better, but sometimes I wish she wouldn't. It's like she thinks I'm a decent person at heart. And I'm pretty sure she's going to be disappointed when she finds out I'm not even close.

Chapter One:
Actions and Reactions

'MIKHAL,' Mrs Hildebrand says. 'Please, sit down.'

I'm already sitting. I know which chair I'm supposed to sit in – the one on the right of the desk, not the left. Mrs Hildebrand wears glasses and she's partly blind in one eye. If I sit on her left she has to turn her whole head to see me. I'd rather keep a few papers and her PC screen between her gaze and me if I can.

She sighs. 'As much as I like you as a person, Mikhal, I'm getting a little sick of seeing you.'

I nod.

'This isn't about the incident with Andrew,' she says. 'At least, it's not *just* about that incident, though it's the most serious one so far. Andrew's going to need stitches, and fighting with another student – whether it's on school premises or not – will not be tolerated.'

'He deserved it. He told me –'

She holds up a hand, cutting off my explanation. 'I don't want to hear that he started it, Mikhal.'

Since I was about to say exactly that, I shut up.

She rubs her temples. Obviously, she doesn't care what had really happened. Andrew deserves every bit of pain and blood – and painful stitches – for what he said to me. We'd been put in a group together for music class. Mr Jackson told us to come up with a three minute composition, which we'd be recording in the next lesson.

'I need to be on the drums,' he said, whacking me on the shoulder with the drumstick. 'And you, Miky, you should sing. You've got the most girly voice out of all of us.'

I bristled as he kept it up, tapping me on the head, the ears, the arm. 'I'm not going to sing in front of the class.'

'Why not? Because you're so shy and retiring? Just do it.' Whack, whack, whack.

'I'd rather be on the drums, since you suck at them so much,' I said, grabbing the drumstick off him. He was still holding it tight, and as I wrenched it, it snapped.

'Ooooh, Mr Jackson's not going to be happy! You're going to have to pay for it. Oh well. It's not like your mum can't afford to.' He said this casually, turning away. 'Either that or she could get you a replacement out of one of the charity bins!'

Everyone around us who'd heard what he said laughed, because just like they all know my mum and dad are solicitors, and good ones

– good enough to have a decent amount of money – they all know Mum has been doing charity work lately, running around the Salvos stores and supermarkets. Cassidy Heights is a small place. Almost everyone knows what everyone else is doing.

I'm not an angry person, usually, but when he said that, I saw red. When I was a little kid, I didn't know our family was any different to anyone else's. I didn't give a crap about the size of people's houses or whether they had an indoor pool or not. Nobody else seemed to care that much, either – if Jake or one of my other friends wanted a swim, or wanted to play the Playstation on a big screen, they'd just come over to my place. If we wanted to kick a ball around, or pretend to be secret agents, or whatever, we'd go to their places. Andrew was one of those friends, too.

But I realised, when I got older, that this stuff actually did matter. People can wish they had what you had, and can hate you for having it when they didn't.

And since the snowstorm a few weeks ago, I realised they hate you even more when you try to help them out. It's so stupid. I know money doesn't come from nowhere. You have to work hard for it, like my mum and dad do.

All this went through my mind as I looked at Andrew's stupid face. He was my friend, but in that moment, it really didn't seem like it. He wasn't even laughing like the others.

During the snowstorm, the roof of Andrew's parents' house had collapsed. They'd lost a lot of their clothes and Andrew's computer and stuff. They had trouble with the insurance – his dad was late with some payments last year or something – and though the electricity had been put back on, they couldn't pay all the repairs, so they didn't have running hot water yet. Mum had taken a box of clothes and canned tomato soup over to their house, since she knew his parents so well from all the sleepovers and birthday parties we'd shared as kids.

And, obviously, Andrew wasn't exactly grateful. That hard-eyed glare he gave me told me he thought it was somehow my fault. I didn't know how I could prove to him I wasn't just being arrogant.

So I hit him.

And I guess that was the straw that broke the camel's back. Or the straw that split his lip, or something, because here I am, back in Mrs Hildebrand's office for the seventh time since, well, since I started counting the times I've been sent here.

'It's about your overall performance at school. Mr Jackson has good reports about your work in Music, but you don't seem to want to apply it. Your class-work is sloppy. You don't get good marks on your assignments. You rarely do homework. You do want to pass, don't you? You don't *want* to be kept down?'

'No,' I say. I don't. I really don't.

'Well, at the rate you're going, you'll be lucky if you don't fail.'

My shock shows in my face. I know, because her gaze instantly turns softer. 'Look.' She pushes her glasses up and leans forwards. That gaze I was avoiding settles right on me. I shift uncomfortably. 'Mr Jackson has put in a good word for you, and it's not impossible. There are programs for young people like you at TAFE. You might want to consider an alternative program – something in technology studies, or an apprenticeship –'

'No!' It just bursts out. It's Mrs Hildebrand's turn to look shocked. 'I – I mean – I'm not a – I'm not *slow*. I don't have a learning disability or anything.'

'I'm not saying that you do,' she says carefully. 'I'm just suggesting that you might benefit from doing something outside of school, something to balance the load, you see?'

I don't, not really.

'If you can find something that you're interested in, something to focus on, and you're willing to work at it, I think it will really help you.'

Oh.

'It won't mean you don't have to do your schoolwork, okay? But if you enrol in a vocational program, we'll be able to negotiate credits.'

I sigh. 'Okay.'

'Do some research,' she goes on, satisfied that I'm taking her seriously. 'Find something you can be passionate about. We'll take it from there. Okay?'

'Okay,' I say meekly. Mrs Hildebrand is satisfied. She smiles.

'Now, I've also arranged for you to work with a student tutor in your class. She can act as your mentor and make sure your work is up to standard.'

'Who is it?'

'Don't look so worried. I just think it might be easier for you to work with someone your own age during class time. Now, I don't ever want you in my office again, Mikhal. You're too smart for this.'

***

'Miky!'

I dodge to one side. I know that voice well enough to know that the best response is to duck and cover. Sure enough, Keira the whirlwind dives past me, just missing me with her backpack. Keira Leichman isn't big, but she likes to hit people more than girls usually do. I'm all for equality of the sexes, but not when it involves me getting clobbered over the head.

'Where were you in History? You left me alone with Mr Morris and his droning voice, and I didn't have anyone's folder to scribble on.

It was boring.'

There are birds in the trees on the other side of the bus shelter. Heaps of them, and they're loud.

'The Andrew thing . . .' I mutter.

'Oh.' The light goes out of her face. Keira's got a history with Andrew – they went out for a bit, but Andrew was an idiot, and they broke up pretty quickly. He's not her favourite person, either. 'You're not getting suspended, are you?'

Keira's changed; I realise. She's always been energetic, but she used to be kind of flaky. During the snowstorm, though, she broke her ankle. She spent a couple of weeks out of school after that. When she came back, her ankle had healed completely – like it had never been broken at all – and there was something . . . deeper about her.

And I had plenty of time to notice. She's been spending a lot of time with my mum, helping out with this charity drive stuff. She still laughs and jokes. She still runs around like a crazy person. But now she does it with a *purpose.*

'No,' I say, and she sighs with relief. The birds screech even more loudly.

'So, anyway, you have to meet my friend. He's staying here for a while.'

She grabs my shoulders to spin me around. 'Hey! Aaron!' she yells in my ear.

Aaron. Yep, it's the boy I saw at the reception desk. He looks just as strange and out-of-place in the school grounds as he did there. But when he sees Keira he smiles, and it's a real smile; I can tell he's happy to see her.

'Aaron, this is Mikhal, he's awesome. Mikhal, this is Aaron.'

'Hi,' I say, holding out a hand. He shies away like I've moved to hit him, and I'm thinking – wow, has word of my violent explosion spread that far already?

Keira doesn't notice. Or if she does, she does a good job of hiding it by changing the subject. 'You'll have to go to Mikhal's place and play *Revenge of the Living Dead* on the 50 inch plasma,' she tells Aaron. To me, she says: 'He's totally into zombie shoot-em-ups.'

'Great,' I return, faking the enthusiasm. Suddenly, though, I'm hit with a wave of loneliness. It's ages since I've hung out with Keira and everyone. 'Hey, we should go to the mall. A few rounds at the arcade would be great.'

Keira looks at Aaron. 'We've gotta go,' she says slowly, and I can tell she's being careful. 'But some other time, right? I'll be at your place on Saturday, anyway. Your mum has more charity stuff to sort.'

'Yeah. Okay.'

My whole plan to avoid going home and dealing with the fallout from today's explosion evaporates as they vanish into the crowd.

'Hey, Mikhal.'

I turn around and find Sharna Devon standing behind me. 'Oh, hi.' I edge away. I don't really want to talk to her. I'm not in the mood for a lecture on the threats to the Great Barrier Reef.

'Mrs Hildebrand asked me to speak to you,' she says, following me. 'You need tutoring?'

'Um, no,' I say. 'I mean, yeah, I guess. But I –'

'Well, we'll get started on Monday, okay? I'm in all your classes anyway, except for Drama, so it'll work out great.'

'Really?' I groan inwardly. I don't exactly hate Sharna, but there are a thousand other people I'd rather spend the day with.

'Yeah!' She grins enthusiastically. 'And we can do some work in the evenings, too, right? I'll make sure you're getting all your homework done. You'll be getting great marks in no time.' She looks up at the birds in the trees, distractedly, and frowns, murmuring: 'It's strange for there to be so many magpies around at this time of year . . .'

'Great.' Could this day get any better? I feel like banging my head on a brick wall. Then, suddenly, an idea hits me. 'Oh, hey, you know? That English essay about 'Something that's important to you'. I haven't even started yet.'

Her eyes light up like I've given her a present. 'Perfect! We can start right now!'

I nod. 'Yeah. Perfect.'

***

Sure enough, when we get home, Mum's sitting at the kitchen table waiting for me. I miss the way she spent so much time at work she was hardly ever at home. I miss the way she used to bury herself in her study whenever she *was* home.

'Mikhal,' she says, then notices I'm not alone. 'Oh. Hello.'

'Mum, this is Sharna.' I lead her into the kitchen, and she looks around, reminding me of an owl with her unblinking eyes. 'She's going to be my *tutor*.'

Mum looks suspicious. 'Oh. I see.'

'We're going to get started right away,' I tell her, edging out of the room. 'I've got an English essay.'

Mum stands up and catches me just before I get to the door. 'I think we should have a family dinner tonight,' she says quietly.

I nearly choke. 'Um –' The last time we ate at the table together I'd cooked a dinner for her birthday because I'd heard her complaining on the phone the night before, to one of her gardening club friends that she missed her mum's tuna rice casserole.

I spent ages preparing it. I'm not really a culinary chef. I'd propped my laptop on the kitchen bench and listened to some British dude's YouTube instructions. It came out a bit blackened at the edges, and I think I used too much rice and it ran over the sides in the oven and stuck to the element, so the kitchen smelled like garlic for three days. Anyway, it turned out I should have set a place at the table for her Blackberry, though, because she spent the whole meal talking to a client about injunctions and cross claims.

She didn't eat a bite of the tuna rice casserole.

'We've got some things to discuss when your dad gets home,' she goes on, interrupting my thoughts. 'So I thought we'd get some pizzas delivered.'

'Pizza?' She's all surprises tonight. 'Sure. Okay.' And then I turn to Sharna, who's paused just outside the door, waiting for me but politely not paying attention. 'Sharna, you like pizza, right?'

Mum glares at me, knowing exactly what I'm doing, and I feel bad. I really do, especially when Sharna leaps on the invitation like a starving person. 'I'm vegan. But Pizza Place does a cheese-free option.'

We go into the lounge room to work. I choose this room because that's where the Playstation is, and as soon as we sit down I sign into *Third Planet Invasion*. 'You can play on Baz's user account,' I tell her. 'He's got a crap score, so you can boost him up –'

'What do you want to do your essay on?' she interrupts, opening a folder on the coffee table. 'I'll tell you a secret – if you choose something you're interested in, it makes it so much easier. You can write as much as you want and then just cut it down.'

I stare at her, astounded. 'Why would I write *more* than what I have to?'

'Because . . .' she shakes her head, just as bewildered as I am, but for different reasons. 'Anyway. What do you really care about?'

'Um . . . zombie games.' I say. 'Hey! I could compare two really great games –'

'I don't think that's deep enough. It's not going to give you much room to explore.'

I sigh and look back at the screen. My guy is getting murdered by rabid zombies, and there's a lot of blood and gore, but somehow I get the feeling Sharna isn't going to let me take a break to rescue him before we've even started working.

'What about your mum and dad's legal work? You could look into what they do with their clients . . .'

'Yeah, but I *don't* care about that. It's boring. It's really, really, boring.'

Sharna sighs, exasperated, and I wonder if she's having second thoughts about tutoring me.

I try to reign in my boredom as I get my laptop from my room and start tapping in a few words. Sharna leans in over my shoulder. 'Are you sure you want to start like that?' It's safe to say that by the time the doorbell rings, I'm already over this whole tutoring thing. 'Gotta get that!' I leap up so fast you'd think the house was on fire. Downstairs, I'm grateful to see that the delivery guy is my friend Donnie.

He's already heard about me being sent to the Principal's office again – I guess everyone's talking about it – and asks for details.

'Dude,' I whisper. 'I'm dying here. Mum's never been this weird before. She's not yelling, or anything. I think she's planning to kill me and bury my body under one of her rosebushes.'

'Don't worry,' Donnie gives a knowing wink. 'Double Pepperoni with extra cheese and a small vegan-veggie-tasteless-special. I put in a box of Dipsticks as well. You'll be set to face anything after that.'

Never ask a pizza delivery boy for life advice.

He shrugs. 'I'd stay and help you out, man, be a buffer or whatever, but I've got three more runs to make and if the pizzas don't arrive on time, hot, and with a smile, I get docked.'

I tell him to get lost then. 'I've got a friend around, anyway.'

He looks past me and through the arched door to the living room he sees Sharna sitting on the couch. He raises his eyebrows.

'She's tutoring me,' I explain, and roll my eyes. Donnie gives me a sympathetic look before he leaves, and I tell Sharna to come and eat.

Mum's waiting for us in the dining area of the kitchen. She's even lit the old-fashioned wood stove. The crackling fire makes the room seem warm and comfy in a way it hasn't for a long time. 'Harry?' she calls.

Dad has super-tuned hearing, which I think comes from twenty years of listening to clients mutter their secrets on the witness stand. He once heard me flushing a piece of Grandma's disgusting three-bean pie down the ensuite toilet in one of the guest bedrooms at the other end of the house.

He'd made me clean all three bathrooms under Anna's supervision. And Anna doesn't let a speck of soap scum pass her inspection.

So he arrives a few moments later, and sits down next to Mum, leaving me to face them like I'm on trial. And poor Sharna is left sitting on the end. She doesn't look uncomfortable, which is good, but I can't help feeling that she must know she's here to be a buffer, not because I actually want her.

They're both silent, so I reach for a piece of pizza, which smells darn good. Dad chooses that moment to clear his throat. I take my hand back guiltily.

'So, Sharna,' he says. 'I knew your mother. It's nice of you to help Mikhal out.'

'Oh, I don't mind. I don't have a very busy schedule.' She speaks in the way my parents like people to speak – concise, polite. I can feel them radiating approval.

'Still, it's very generous of you to volunteer your time. Mikhal has certain problems with –'

'Hang on,' I burst in. 'I'm sitting right here!'

'Mikhal,' he says levelly. 'You know we love you, and we want the best for you.'

I nod. Nothing good ever follows a sentence like that.

'We had a call from your school today,' Mum jumps in. I can tell this is it. The floodgates are open now, and nothing's going to hold them back, not even Sharna's presence. 'They're very concerned about your performance.'

I nod again, waiting for it.

'Bad marks –' explodes Mum. 'That's bad enough, but –'

'Fighting?' Dad splutters. 'I would have thought better of you.'

'If you can't control yourself around other students –'

'I thought we'd bought you up knowing –'

'About conflict resolution.'

'Putting a boy in hospital? I'm ashamed of you, Mikhal. You and Andrew used to be friends. What happened?'

I could tell them so many things, but I don't think my words will be heard under this barrage.

Finally, Dad says: 'Mrs Hildebrand made some helpful suggestions.'

'Dad,' I say carefully and calmly. 'I don't really need to do that stuff. I promise I'll work harder. I'll do my homework. I'll go to all my classes. And Sharna . . .'

I look across at her, and see that she's frozen, her hands on the edge of the table. Her lips are pinched.

I feel like an absolute tool for putting her in the middle of this.

'Mikhal, you know that's not going to be enough. I really think there's something to this.

That's what your mum and I have been talking about.'

'This is what we've decided,' Mum says. 'You'll help me out with the charity drive. Volunteer work is such a rewarding experience, Miky. You can really make a difference.'

I glare at her. 'You want me to sell hotdogs outside the church? How is that supposed to help my schoolwork?'

'It's not forever,' she tells me quietly. 'And Mrs Hildebrand agreed it was a good idea.'

'It's community service! They make criminals do shit like that –'

'Miky! Watch your mouth!' she snaps. 'You could have been expelled. Or worse. Andrew's parents had every right to press charges.'

'They wouldn't,' I mutter. 'They know who you are.'

'That's enough!' Dad slaps the table. 'You're doing this, and if it doesn't teach you to fly straight and take some responsibility for your actions and your life, nothing will.'

Dad's good at making speeches. He loves it, especially if he can make it sound like he's smart and philosophical. He *is* smart and philosophical, of course, but that's beside the point, and the point is that speeches are completely useless in the real world. You can't fix everything by stringing a load of long words together. You can't fix *me*.

'Look,' Mum says, sounding calm and collected now that Dad's the one playing Bad Cop.

'We'll work this out, okay? There are plenty of options. We'll just find one that suits you.'

I swallow all my angry protests and nod because there's nothing I can say that they will actually listen to.

Dad smiles tightly. He takes a slice of pizza, puts it on a plate, leans over to rub my shoulder, and leaves the room.

Mum takes out her Blackberry.

'So,' Sharna says. 'You could do your essay on charities! That would be ideal. You could look at the different ways people are receiving help . . .'

I sigh and start shovelling pizza into my mouth. It's already cold.

***

My room is my sanctuary. It's on the third floor, which is a converted attic, fitted under the roof so the ceiling slopes and my band posters keep falling off it. Fall Out Boy has a rip down the centre, and Brand New sags alarmingly. Blink 182 – old-school, but nevertheless worthy – spends more time on the floor than in it's rightful place above the Silversun Pickups, and next to Alter Ego.

I have a pact with Anna that while she can vacuum my floor or change my sheets any time she wants, she doesn't touch my desk.

She says she doesn't get paid enough to reconstruct a bomb site anyway.

It works out well for both of us.

She's in there when I climb the stairs after finally getting Sharna to go home. She's hanging a few shirts in the wardrobe.

'There's pizza in the fridge,' I tell her. 'If you want some. And anyway, shouldn't you be home?'

She raises an eyebrow. 'Trouble?'

'What else?'

She smiles gently and changes the subject. 'How's Roger?'

For my birthday, Mum wanted to get me a new laptop. Instead, I got her to take me to the music shop in the mall. They don't like me in there because I was always going in there to look at the green guitar and not buying anything.

Ron, the owner, was overjoyed to finally sell him to me. Roger is second hand and a shiny green. I knew as soon as I saw him that I needed that guitar. And even though there is a scuff mark on the fret board, and the previous owner somehow felt the need to draw a little smiley face above the input jack, I knew it was my guitar.

Roger hooks up nicely to my stereo system. He sits there, waiting for me to play him. But I haven't had the courage yet.

'Good.' I say this earnestly. 'He's good. I'm . . . not so much.'

'Hey,' she slaps my hand. 'None of that. I've heard you play.'

'I don't know,' I say. 'I'm just too scared. But I replaced the pickups and I got a new strap . . .'

'I'll pretend I know what you're talking about,' Anna says. 'Anyway, he looks handsome.'

I change the subject. 'You're not usually here this late.'

'Your mum is letting me put in a few extra hours. I'm a bit strapped for cash at the moment. Lily – there's this special school. They cater to kids with severe disabilities. If I had enough to cover the fees –'

Lily is Anna's daughter. She was born with a weak heart and all kinds of health problems. She needs constant care. Even though she never complains, I know it must be really hard for Anna to deal with.

'Better get back to it,' she says with a smile. 'Just be good, okay, Miky? This will all work out.'

I smile at her, because no matter what my problems are, hers are so much worse, and I feel selfish being miserable about them.

She leaves, flicking off the light as she goes because she knows I prefer the dark. I look at Roger in the light coming from my laptop screen. I grab my notebook out of my pocket and flick it open to my latest song. I wrote this one for Roger.

But I can't do it, not tonight. I pick up Old Faithful, the acoustic guitar I've had since forever, and strum out a tune.

It's easy to create music.

'Music is a force,' Mr Jackson is always telling us in music class. 'It's powerful enough to make you feel and remember. It's a formidable tool.'

He always says things like that, and he sounds kind of half-crazy when he does, but I can see exactly what he means every time I pick up my guitar or sing a few lines of a song.

If only life was made up of notes and melody, the way songs are. I could just cross it out and rewrite it all. Only better.

Chapter Two:
Bridges

IT'S Charity Day.

I stopped thinking of Saturdays as Saturdays a few weeks ago, when our house stopped being a house and started being Charity Collection Headquarters. On Saturdays, every bag and box of donated goods in Cassidy Heights ends up in our garage, and the Charity Mums show up to sort them, catalogue them, and drive them all over town.

'No!'

Mum storms in. If there was a cartoon thundercloud hanging over her head, shooting little lightning bolts, she couldn't look more angry.

'I labelled those boxes specifically. They were supposed to go to the city centre.'

'I'm sorry,' Nina says. Nina is engaged to my friend Jake's dad. She's the one who started all this charity stuff, so I guess I can blame her for it all . . . but I can't help liking her anyway. She's always kind and she puts up with my mum snapping at her like it's no big deal, like she gets that Mum doesn't really mean it. 'It's my fault. I left Hayley in charge. That box was with all the others. When the truck showed up, she just told them to load everything.'

Mum sighs. 'It's the second time it's happened.'

'It's not the end of the world,' Nina says, pausing for a moment to pat her stomach.

'Oh, would you please sit down for a minute, at least?' Mum scolds her. 'You're making me nervous.'

Nina smiles. She's been doing that a lot, and it suits her. But I think she's had enough of people hovering around her. 'Don't be ridiculous! I'm pregnant, not dying. There's so much work to do . . .'

Mum spies me. 'Mikhal, you can go and help Keira in the garage for a while, can't you?'

'I was going to go and see Baz –'

Mum gives me a Look. It's the kind of Look that needs a capital 'L', the kind you don't argue against.

I head for the garage.

It's a big garage. It fits six cars, but Mum usually parks her Jeep in the driveway, and Dad's Mercedes is never here because neither is he. I used to be able to skateboard in here. Not anymore though; every inch of it is boxes and crates and those big garbage bags, and tables with folded clothes and cans of food and blankets, and all kinds of the junk that turns up in charity bins.

It smells.

It's not a bad smell. It's just a smell of a hundred different people, and households, and materials all rolled into one. It's the smell of dust, and mildew, and blankets that have been folded up in cupboards for too long. Even with the door open and a cold breeze blowing in, it's almost overpowering.

My lip curls up. There are a thousand things I'd rather be doing than *this*.

There are two other people in the garage, folding clothes into two piles. Keira and Aaron.

'Nina's got a load of boxes in her car,' Keira says. 'We just need to bring them in. Aaron, you want to help us?'

Aaron looks up and gives her a single nod. How can anyone look so serious all the time?

Keira nudges me. 'Don't look so down. It'll be over before you know it.'

I follow her through the garage door to Nina's car. It's parked next to Mum's neatly-trimmed box hedge, and there's another group of those damn magpies screeching like it's a football match. Not loudly enough to cover the raised voices of a man and a woman who are arguing over a tarp-covered trailer, though.

'It's due back at the rental place at lunch time,' she's saying. 'You should have told me you needed it longer.'

'I was going to leave earlier! I got held up –' he replies, exasperated. I've seen them before, two more of Mum and Nina's recruits; and I wonder how they sold this charity stuff to them, since neither of the sound too enthusiastic right now.

'You know, it seems like no one knows what anyone's doing,' I murmur to Kiera and Aaron. 'Who's in charge, anyway?'

'Well, unofficially, it's Nina's gig,' explains Keira. The boot of Nina's car is open and she hoists a box out. 'But now she's pregnant . . .'

'You should take charge,' I point out. 'You're doing more work than most of them.'

'No way!' She laughs. 'I'm the world's most disorganised person. I'm not saying I don't love helping, but I can't be in charge of things. Ever.'

'She sells herself short,' Aaron says quietly. The words come out stiffly, like he's quoting them from a movie. What follows is more natural. 'She would do an excellent job if she allowed herself the chance.'

This is completely true. Keira is the most confident person on the planet. I wonder why she's so reluctant to take the reins on this.

'Just wait a second,' I say, indicating that Keira should put the box she's lifting down for a second. There's a pen in my pocket, along with my notebook. I pull it out and rest it on the nearest box while I scribble. 'Help – charity – goodwill – we need a name that is about what you're doing. Something solid. Honest. Helpful . . . reliable . . . belief . . . *trust*.'

I circle this word.

Keira is staring.

I shrug and keep scribbling. 'You'll need a logo. Something edgy but . . . suave. You want people to think of being included. Like a circle.' I draw a spiralling design, then cross it out. 'Nah, that's not right. Too . . . loopy.' I try again. Two vertical lines, and an arc connecting them. 'Huh.'

'That's good,' Keira says slowly. 'It says 'reaching out', it says 'connecting'. It's a . . . like a . . .'

'Bridge.' Aaron's voice is quiet. 'It's a bridge.'

'Oh yeah!' I'm pretty thrilled that they like what I've done. 'Yeah, that's what it is. You can call it the Bridge Foundation. Or something.'

There's heaps more to talk about as we finish unloading the boxes. Keira gets me thinking when she says 'There are hundreds of people out there that need help. Not just people who got affected by the snowstorm.'

I nod. Lily is up the top of that list. We could raise money for her to go to her special school, and all the kids like her.

There should probably be schedules, I suggest, and rosters so that people know who's working when and where. Then we need to keep track of the donations, and where they're supposed to go, and who's taking them.

I'm just asking Keira to write up a list of the Charity Mums, because I don't know their names, when I realise there's someone watching me from the doorway of the garage.

It's Mum.

***

She's ecstatic. It's like all her dreams have come true. Not only has she solved my vocational problems, she's scored herself another charity volunteer, plus a logo and name.

'You can work the logo up on your laptop,' she gushes. It's late. Everyone else has gone home, and we're going through the last of the boxes from Nina's car. She folds one of Jake's little brother's old hoodies and puts it in a pile. 'We'll get letterheads done up, and we can –'

She frowns for a moment.

'What?' I ask.

'Well, it's just that this is a non-profit organisation. If we want to branch out like that, we probably need financial backing.'

I shrug. 'Can't you fund it?'

'I can do a lot,' she says. 'But if we start pouring all our money into this, we'll eventually run out.'

'So we'll campaign,' I say. 'Doorknocking and stuff. Rattle tin cans in the mall.'

Mum nods uncertainly.

'Well,' I go on, thinking as I'm talking. 'What about something more original? There are other ways to make money. You could hold a fundraiser.'

'A trivia night!' Mum brightens up instantly.

I grimace. 'Trivia nights are fine if you're over eighteen and you can buy scotch over the bar. Otherwise . . . *snore-fest*. What about a concert?'

'A concert.' She repeats the word like it's unfamiliar. I pull out an old pair of jeans, and something that was wrapped up inside them falls out. I bend down to grab it. 'People love music. People will pay to see a good band. And that way, you're not excluding anyone. Everyone can enjoy music.' I bend down to pick it up.

'Miky,' she says, softly. 'I think you might be on to something.'

My heart is thundering. I'm thinking about the concert. Who could we get to play? Most bands won't do stuff for free, especially not big ones. We'd have to pay them a small fee at least.

I looked down at my hands. The thing that fell out is a phone. It's an older model. It must be one of Jake's old ones. I guess it could still be useful. If I got a charger, I could put it in with the donations. It's an old phone, but if I needed a phone and couldn't afford one, I'd be happy enough with one like this. I slip it into my pocket.

***

I practise that night. I record myself onto the laptop, and when I play it back, it sounds all right. I need to work on my pitch. And there's one line in the final song that just doesn't work.

You know, if I thought I could measure up
To anything you wanted me to be
Could, Should, Would –
I'd do it all
My guard is up
Because I'm never what you want to expect
I'm just acting tough
And it's never enough'

I pull out a notepad and write some words. *Want, need, yearn . . . burn.*

For some stupid reason this makes me think of Sharna. The light in her eyes when she was talking about the English essay. The possibilities she sees for making it something really great. Why can't I do that? Why can't I get as excited about school as she can?

I find myself looking at the mobile phone I'd found in Nina's boxes. I put my old guitar aside and rummage through my desk drawers. I've got a hundred old chargers. It's a good thing Anna isn't allowed to throw anything out of my room. I have about three with the right connection.

Plugging it into the wall, it blinks on. It's so flat that only the battery icon comes up. It'll need a while to charge before it'll turn on.

***

I fall asleep and dream that I'm an ant. I don't know why I'm an ant, but I kind of like it for a while. Being small is nice.

But then I realise I'm on stage. And everyone's looking around for me. 'Where's Mikhal?'
they ask.

'I'm here,' I say, but they can't hear me. And
because I'm an ant, I can't reach the strings on
my guitar, either. It's not my old acoustic guitar.
It's Roger, bright green and tantalising. I keep
jumping up and down but it's out of reach . . .
then, one little stick-leg brushes it and it starts
to fall, and there's this clashing, rushing sound
as that little smiley face rushes towards me . . .

I jerk awake. I haven't been asleep long –
only a few minutes. The room is dark, except
for the light coming from the charging mobile
phone. My own phone is set on night mode,
glowing softly blue beside it, showing the time
– 11:04 – but I realise I didn't dream the sound.
The noise is coming from the phone.

It sounds like moving water. A gushing river
or the sea. And wind . . .

It sounds almost like a song.

I pick up the phone. The sound continues,
growing louder and softer, ebbing and flowing.
I can catch that tune, I think. I hum softly. No
words, just a melody . . .

'Are you there?'

I jump. I drop the phone. The charger plug
falls out and it bounces on the floor. The screen
goes dark. The sound stops.

'No,' I whisper, and I hastily plug the phone
back in. The screen stays dark, even when I

mash all the buttons on the keypad. 'No, no, come on . . .'

Nothing.

It's crazy. I didn't hear a voice, of course I didn't. I didn't hear anything. There was no call connected.

But that voice. It was soft and faint. I thought it sounded almost familiar, but I couldn't be sure whose it was. A girl, though. Definitely a girl.

But there's nothing. The phone is dead. I sigh and put it back on my bedside table. I was imagining the whole thing.

Chapter Three:
At the Treehouse

THE next day is Sunday, and I'm planning on having an all-day sleep-in, but my phone starts ringing at quarter to eight. It's an unknown number, a landline, not a mobile. 'Wha?' I mumble.

'Mikhal?'

I'm still scrunching sleep out of my eyes and trying to get my brain to function, but I recognise the voice. 'Jake –?'

'Sorry. Sorry to call you so early. But have you seen my phone? It's a Nokia – I think Nina chucked it in one of the boxes she left at your place for the charity drive –'

'Bridge,' I interrupt him.

'What?'

'Bridge Foundation. At least, I think that's what it's going to be called. I haven't worked out the details yet.'

'. . . Mikhal!' Jake yells. 'My phone!'

'There was one in the boxes. I've got it right here.'

I can hear him turn aside, talking to someone in the background. 'He's got it. Shut up, Daniel – he says he found it.'

It's only then that I remember what happened last night. The phone is still plugged into the charger, but it doesn't look like it's working. The charge light isn't even on. 'I think it's broken. Last night it just started making weird sounds. Like static.'

Jake is silent for a minute. 'Like static?'

'Well, no. Saying I heard static . . . well, that sounds less *weird*. It was more like waves on the ocean, or something. And . . . I thought I heard a voice. It was pretty quiet, and maybe I imagined it, maybe it was noise from the street outside or something, but . . . I don't think so . . . Jake? Are you still there?'

He doesn't say anything for a long moment. When he does speak, his voice was low and urgent. 'I've got to call the others,' he says. 'Mikhal, can you come to my place? And bring the phone?'

'Like I said, it's busted,' I remind him. 'But fine. Since I'm awake now, anyway.'

He misses the sarcasm. 'Thanks. Just get here as soon as you can.' Before he hangs up, I just catch the words: 'No, jeez, Daniel! Just get Keira's number off your phone, okay? Hurry up!'

Keira? What's she got to do with this? And what the hell is going on?

***

'Why don't you ride your bike?' Anna says when I ask if she can take me over to Jake's.

I roll my eyes. 'Please. Dad's not up yet and Mum's still in bed. I'll wash your car.'

She holds up her hands. 'I'll give you a ride if you promise you won't touch my car.'

I hate washing cars, but still, I feel a bit offended.

'How's Lily?' I ask her as we turn onto the main street.

'She's got a thing about dolphins at the moment. Everything's about dolphins. I made her a dolphin costume.' She laughs. 'It's a velvet cloak with some buttons sewn on the hood for eyes and a blowhole. She wants to be a . . .' She stops for a moment, and frowns.

'Marine Biologist?' I guess.

She's tight-lipped and I know exactly what she's thinking, because I'm thinking the same thing.

She drops me at the curb. Jake is waiting for me on the front porch. I've only been to his house a few times, but on each occasion I've done a double-take at his neighbour's yard. Mrs Henders is crazy and old. She has freaky taste. Am I imagining things or does she have more pink flamingos standing on her lawn than last time?

'Where is it?' Jake says.

'Hey!' I hold up my hand. 'Nice to see you, too, mate.'

He walks towards me. I give him the phone, and the charger I dug up. He grabs it, hits the power button. Nothing. His face falls.

'Jake?'

He looks up, his face grim, determined.

'The others are waiting. Come on,' he says.

'Others?' I was expecting Keira, but 'others' sounds like it's going to be a crowd.

Jake leads the way. We cross the street to Phoenix Park. I didn't grow up in Cassidy Heights like Jake and Keira did, so I've only been to the park a few times to play soccer. Jake knows his way around, though. He heads straight past the pond and the pagoda, which is covered in plastic to keep the weather out, and into the darkness of the pine plantation on the far side.

The trees close over us. It's like walking into a cave. It's cold outside, but it's colder under here, where the sun hasn't reached. I see a couple of rust-stained warning signs telling people to keep out, but we keep going till we reach a particular tree. There's a ladder nailed to the trunk, leading up to a pretty decent treehouse.

Keira is standing at the bottom, and so is someone else – Aaron. Daniel, Jake's younger brother, is leaning over the edge of the tree-house platform. They all look pretty serious.

'What's this?' I laugh. 'The Secret Seven?'

'We don't have a secret password yet,' calls Daniel. 'I wanted it to be 'velociraptor', but we're the only people who come here anyway.'

Jake shakes his head with a grimace.

Keira, for once, isn't smiling. 'You've got the phone?' she asks.

Jake holds it up. 'It's not working. But Mikhal . . . let's go up.'

He motions to the ladder, and I climb it carefully. At the top is a wide platform covered by a slanted, wooden roof. It's a bit rickety, but it doesn't seem in danger of falling right this second. I don't think I've ever been in a real treehouse before. 'Did you build this?'

'Yep,' Daniel says proudly. 'We've fixed it up a bit since then.'

I look around. 'Why aren't there any birds?' Those magpies have been everywhere. You'd think there'd be hundreds up here, where there's so many trees. But it's almost dead silent, and I can hear whispers from down below. Keira, saying: 'Are you sure this is the right thing to do?'

Then Jake. 'He's either going to think we're insane and take off, or he can help us. If he actually heard . . .'

'Is it really possible?' Aaron's unfamiliar quiet voice. 'It's been a long time . . .'

'Just go up. I want to hear what he's got to say.' Jake says decisively.

The others climb up behind me and the platform shifts as they sit down in a ragged circle.

Jake puts the phone in the centre, and suddenly everyone's eyes are focused on it, staring like it's the Holy Grail or something.

'Mikhal,' Jake says. 'We've got something to tell you.'

'I *did* hear a voice, didn't I?' I pump a fist in the air. 'I *knew* it.'

'If you did, it's a good thing,' Jake says. 'I really, really hope you did.'

'Why? Who was it? It sounded like a girl.'

Keira takes over. 'It was Cari. Rebecca. You remember Rebecca?'

Yeah, I remember Rebecca, the exchange student Jake had staying with him for a few days a couple of weeks ago. I only met her once, when she came with us to the movies and the mall one night. She had a thing with Jake. They'd made a pretty good couple, I thought. She was quiet and private, like him. But there was something . . . about her . . . I can't quite put words to it.

I look at Aaron, and I realise that he looks a little bit like she did, or like she would, if she had a bit more colour to her. Not quite as pale and ethereal, but almost. 'Are you her brother?' I ask. 'Cousin?'

'Not exactly,' Aaron says. 'But she's very important to us all.'

No one really seems to know what to say next. It's Daniel who breaks the silence.

'Aaron's not his real name. He's from another world, and so is Cari. Rebecca.'

'Another world.' I repeat this, frowning. Is this just some huge joke they're playing on me? I try to play along. 'You mean, like, aliens?'

'More like . . . another dimension. A world that exists beside ours. It's connected in places.'

'By bridges,' Keira says.

'Bridges.' Yeah, Mikhal. Keep repeating everything. Maybe hearing it in your own voice will make it make sense. 'Bridges?'

'They're unstable. They shift and move from one place to another.' Keira continues. 'I crossed one.'

She's not laughing. She should be laughing, shouldn't she? People don't talk about stuff like this without laughing. Not unless they're in a movie, or a book, or crazy in the friggin' head . . .

'I went to Shar. It's this fantastic city. It's Cari's – Rebecca's home. It's Archon's home, too, though he's also part human.'

I stare at her.

'Okay,' she says, taking a deep breath. She pulls something out of her pocket. It's a clear crystal. In the spots of light filtering through the pine needles overhead, it glints a hundred different colours. 'I'm going to touch you, Mikhal. Okay?'

'Why?'

She doesn't answer, just reaches over and rests her fingers on my knee.

A shock runs through me. I can see –

I can see a bridge. It leads up into the sky, and as I crane my neck I see it stretches up to a glittering city. It's beautiful, that city. The towering spires and arching bridges are delicate, like lace. Like they shouldn't be able to hold themselves up, they're so fragile . . .

Colours surround people. The colours drift around their bodies, red, gold, violet . . . the colours mean something. They pulsate, like feelings, and sometimes they change from one colour to another . . .

And then I'm there, walking through one of the streets, people on either side of me. They're tall and sinewy, and they don't look too friendly. Rashae. The name comes to me as if I've known it for a while. Guardian Rashae – and I'm afraid of her, and angry at her, and . . .

She hates me. She hates us. I can feel how much she despises humans, how she thinks we're vile, disgusting, repulsive creatures.

And my ankle. My ankle should hurt, but I can walk on it without feeling pain and it's amazing . . .

And then I'm lying on a bed. There's an old man beside me. He is talking in a gravelly voice . . .

Faces, many of those cold, pale faces bending over me . . . the crystal, the same one in Keira's hand right now, is in the hands of one of them . . .

A telescope. A bronze telescope, heavy in my hands. Not just the actual weight of it. It means something, this telescope. People are afraid of it. The Guardians have it, and they're going to use it – we're in danger – the ice, the snowstorm, *this can happen, and worse . . . they **hate** us, humans, they're so scared of us, and what we can do. If they wipe us out, they'll be safe . . .*

A rushing river of light. The vinarhi . . . Rebecca. A mobile phone clutched in her outstretched hands as she tries to reach my hands, her face alive with panic and fear. . . and the crystal shard, in my hands (Keira's hands) slashing downwards, cutting a golden thread, and Rebecca is gone and Keira is here and –

I am here, back in myself, breathing heavily.

'Sorry,' Keira says. I can't see her because my vision is grey and blurred. 'It's always a bit much to take in the first time. I tried to be gentle, but . . . just breathe slowly. Do you think I shared too much at once?'

This last bit isn't aimed at me, obviously, because I'm pressing my head to my knees and trying not to throw up. Aaron answers. 'He needed to know. I've seen enough of your world now to know how hard it is for your people to believe. You made it easier for him.'

Easier. Well, yeah, it is that. I can't exactly *not* believe them now I've had Keira's memories downloaded directly into my brain.

Archon. Aaron. Cari – Rebecca. Of course they're from another world. Neither of them belongs here. And Keira's miraculous recovery – it was impossible in our world. But not in this other one.

'Okay,' I say, gulping and raising my head. Just a little, because everything seems to hurt right now. 'Okay, so there's a city in the sky. And there are Bridges to that city. And there are places in between. And Rebecca – Cari – is still trapped there. And . . . and Jake's phone can connect with her.'

'She has my phone, actually,' Keira says. 'The connection was open when we came through. But when I cut the thread, we lost all contact with her. Jake's been trying to get it back for ages, but the phone is useless. It won't even make normal calls.'

'I had to buy a new phone. I think that's why Nina thought I meant to chuck my old one out, and she put it in that box to donate.' Jake says. 'But somehow you've managed to make it work. What were you doing just before the phone turned on?'

'Sleeping!' I say. It's not like I was doing anything special like playing with a magic crystal. 'I was sleeping and having some stupid dream. Maybe that's it.' But no, that's not all. 'I'd just finished . . . I was playing . . . and singing.'

Oh, man. I never, never admit to anyone what I do with my music. My face burns.

'Um – you can't tell anyone,' I say.

They're all looking at me, and I'm sure I can tell what they're thinking. *Mikhal? He can't sing.* I bet they're laughing on the inside.

'Wait a minute. I'm sitting with a bunch of people who think there's a glowing city in the sky!' I burst out, glaring at each of them, daring them to say what they're thinking to my face. 'And one of them thinks he's come from another world.'

'I don't just think it,' Aaron says. 'I was born there. But I'm half-human, because my father crossed over and met my mother in Shar. I'm living with Mrs Henders while I work out how to return.'

'That's not the point – or maybe it is. It's all crazy, the whole thing! And you're seriously judging *me?*'

'Mikhal, we didn't say anything!' Keira butts in. 'I just didn't know you were into music.'

'I'm not. I mean, I just muck around sometimes. I'm not, like, good, or anything.'

'Could that be it, though? You singing?' Jake looks at Aaron, or Archon. 'Could that make the connection?'

'I don't know, exactly,' he replies thoughtfully. 'We don't –'

'You don't really have music in Shar, do you?' Keira says. 'I never heard any.'

'We don't play it openly, like you do in your world. It's closely-monitored by the Guardians. And it certainly doesn't have the same sounds. The same . . . lack of restraint.'

'Yes! Music is all about resonouncing!' Daniel says, making up his own words as his voice rises with excitement. 'Isn't that what your crystal does, Keira?'

'Resonances,' Keira corrects him. 'And yeah . . . the crystals in Shar respond to resonances. I think people's auras do, too, since the crystals can be trained to respond to particular people. I mean, yeah, there definitely could be a link.'

'The music teacher at school, Mr Jackson,' I say slowly, 'says that music makes connections between things. I always thought that was a cool idea, and it kind of makes sense. Music can make you feel something you didn't even know you could feel, or remember things you thought you'd forgotten. You can touch people with music. You know? That's how it is for me, anyway.'

I'm kind of embarrassed saying this. Even though I think it's true, it sounds kind of fruity.

'That sounds like a very . . . Sharian thing to say,' Keira says, glancing at Aaron. 'They're all about things affecting other things.'

Jake nods, too, like he knows what I'm talking about. 'It kind of makes sense. But if the music did that, somehow made the connection, then we have to try it again. It might be our only way to save Cari.'

Save Cari. Of course. She's the Princess in the tower. And the whole bunch of evil witches are the Guardians.

'Is this for real?' I ask them.

No one answers that.

Chapter Four:
Making Connections

WE TAKE a bus to my house and my nerves are fluttering. I've never played in front of anyone else. Now they're all going to witness my failure.

Mum is in the lounge room, organising papers on the coffee table. 'Oh, hello!' she looks up, surprised to see everyone trooping in. 'I didn't know you were bringing friends over, Mikhal. I'll get Anna to cut some cake for you –'

'Can't stop, Mum!' I tell her, ready to barrel past up to my room. 'Got important stuff to do.'

'Hi, Mrs Wright,' Keira says, giving me a look that says I'm being rude, and I bristle, thinking about how important this is and desperately not wanting to waste any time. 'I'd love some cake, but we'll get it ourselves.'

'You'll make her suspicious if you say stuff like that,' Keira whispers to me as she brushes past me into the kitchen. 'Besides, I want to talk to Anna.'

We've got no choice but to follow her.

Anna is in the kitchen, wiping down the

benches. While Keira chats to her, Aaron looks around the kitchen, wonder in his eyes.

'You've seen a kitchen before, right?' I ask quietly.

'Not one like this,' he marvels.

'Mum had it remodelled last year. I don't know why. Anna's the only one who uses it, and she doesn't really care what model dishwasher we have.'

'I wish I could show this to my sister,' he says quietly so Anna won't hear. 'This whole world is full of wonders.'

'You've got a sister?'

He nods. 'Arina. She – and my mother, Sarinne – are in trouble. We left them in Shar. I'm worried about what the Guardians will do to them.'

'They won't kill them or anything, though.' I say, then instantly wonder if it's true. 'Right?'

'I don't know. I'm hoping they are safe, but until I see them again, I can't be sure they're unharmed.'

I eye him closely. 'That first day I saw you at school, outside the Principal's office,' I say slowly. 'You were talking to Sharna. You touched her hand and then told her the papers she was missing were in her drawer. Did you read her mind?'

'It's called the *ihlwarh*,' he reminds me. 'I didn't mean to use it on her. It's not supposed to work with most humans, but I have a feeling that when the Ether calls strongly to someone, it allows a connection. She – Sharna – worries a lot. She feels she's not doing well enough.'

'Really?' I remember how I'd been sure there was something bothering her. But how can she be worried about not doing well enough? She's every teacher's favourite student. She gets great marks. And she's so confident and sure of herself. Could Aaron be wrong? 'Keira said you're part human. Maybe that's why it worked.'

'I don't think so. Cari was able to share *ihlwarh* with Jake, and she doesn't share blood with people of your world. Besides, the part of me that is human – I don't know it well,' he says regretfully. 'My father was . . . taken away . . . when I was very young. But I might still have relatives on your world. Somewhere.'

He looks wistful, and I can tell this is something he's longed for. I think I can understand it. He must feel lonely, here, stranded among strangers and away from the only family he's ever known.

'What was his name?' I ask. 'Your dad, I mean.'

'It was a strange name – among our people. I always liked the sound of it, though. I would repeat it to myself when I lay awake at night, thinking about him. He was called Frederick Mason.'

'AAAiiigh!'

It's Anna who'd screamed. She jumps backwards, dropping the cake on the floor. Crumbs burst all over the clean tiles. It takes me a while to figure out what's happening, but then

I see it – a mouse, crouched in the corner under the cupboards. It's twitching its whiskers, unsure of which way to go.

Keira lunges for the bench, and then I realise there's another one, and she's got it in her hands. 'Whoo! Gotcha!' she crows.

A third one scurries out from under the fridge, sees the commotion and darts back into shelter.

'Don't worry,' Keira says to the mouse she's caught. 'I'll take you outside.'

'Where did they all come from?' Anna shakes her head. She's practically standing on tip-toes, face twisted in disgust. 'We've never had mice in here before!'

Keira takes her captive outside and releases it. When we're all upstairs in my room, with a pile of cake on a plate and glasses of orange juice, I close the door to make sure no one can interrupt us. Then I close the curtains and we all find spaces to sit on the floor.

'That's a cool guitar,' Daniel says, looking at Roger.

'It doesn't work.' I lie, suddenly afraid that he'll ask to play it and feeling insanely possessive. I pick up my acoustic guitar instead and perch on the edge of my bed as Jake fiddles with plugging the phone into the wall using my old charger.

Silence falls.

'Okay, so just play whatever it was you played last night,' Keira prompts me. She's holding the crystal in her hands, and I can see it glowing faintly.

For a moment I freeze. I try to remember what I was playing but all I can hear is a noise in my head. It's my blood rushing in my ears.

This is it, I think. I'm actually going to play in front of other people.

They're your friends, I tell myself. *They're not going to judge you.*

But what if it doesn't work? What if I . . . expose myself . . . for no reason?

Then I will.

I sigh and pull the guitar into my lap.

And just like it always happens when I start to play, I'm not sitting there anymore. I'm not even in the room. There's no one around me. I'm somewhere else, somewhere inside the notes, vibrating along with the strings of my guitar and the tones of my voice.

There's the sound of rushing in my ears. At first it's indistinguishable from the blood pounding in my veins, but then I realise it's the same sound I heard last night.

And it's not just me that hears it. Everyone leans forwards, as if that will make the connection stronger. The crystal in Keira's hands is glowing more brightly now.

I keep playing, keep singing. I can't hear what I'm singing. I'm not paying attention to what my fingers are doing. I let the music make itself, working in with the sound coming from the phone.

' sshhh . . .'

It's a voice – is it a voice?

'. . . wish you could hear me . . .'

'Cari!' Jake yells.

'Shh!' hisses Keira, but it's too late.

There's a knock at the door. 'Is everything okay in there?'

We all jump. Keira hides the crystal. It's Anna's voice, and I know she won't come in unless I ask her to, but the moment is gone. The phone is dark. We all look guiltily at one another, as if we've been busted breaking the rules, even though I'm pretty sure there's no rules for what we're doing.

'Fine,' I call, annoyed.

We listen until her footsteps recede, then we all breathe a sigh of relief. 'Anna is working more hours,' I say. 'She's around a lot more than she used to be.'

'This isn't going to work,' Keira says. 'We need to go somewhere no one will interrupt us.'

We might only get one chance at this. We might not even get one, unless we're lucky. What happened last night might have been a complete fluke. But just in case it does work, we don't want anyone barging in on us while we're trying this. And by that we mean parents.

'There's only one adult we can trust with all this,' Jake tells us, and the others all seem to know who he's talking about.

'Mrs Henders will be more than happy to have you stay,' Aaron says. 'But she will not make excuses for us.'

Chapter Five:
Contact

IT'S Secret Seven all the way; a sleepover party. We're all telling our parents various stories. Mum thinks I'm staying at Jake's. Keira's telling her mum she's staying with a girl in our class, Angelina. 'Mum won't be happy if she knows I'm sleeping over at a boy's house,' she says. Her mum works at a bakery, at odd hours, so she's usually asleep the rest of the time. 'She's been pretty strict since my accident happened, so I'm going to have to clear it with Angie. A few weeks ago I made the mistake of saying I was having dinner at Sharna Devon's place, you know, when I was going out with Baz. She called Sharna's dad. Pfff. Bad idea. She got an earful of swear words from him, so she wasn't in the best mood to start with, and when she found out I was actually at Baz's place . . . oh, boy.'

Jake and Daniel can tell the truth, because now that Aaron lives next door with Mrs Henders, Jake and Daniel are over there a lot, and Nina and Mr Miles have struck up a come-over-for tea-and-biscuits friendship with Mrs Henders. All they have to do is say there's a new Xbox game they need to check out.

Unfortunately, it's a Sunday, so we all need to make promises about getting to school the next day, but luckily it goes down okay with everyone's parents. Except mine.

'You think you deserve a night with your friends?' Mum says. 'Miky, you're still in trouble over this fight.'

'Please, Mum!' I beg her, thinking fast. I can't tell her Keira is sleeping over, or that will raise her doubts. 'Keira is going to come for dinner, and we're need to talk more about this concert for the charity. With Nina. And Jake's going to help out, and so is Keira's friend, Aaron. There's a lot to plan . . .'

Mum is great friends with Nina, but she still looks suspicious.

'Well,' she says at last. 'I am proud of you making such an effort with this. I'll call Mrs Hildebrand tomorrow and see whether you can get credit . . .'

'I don't care about the credit,' I say, and now I'm being completely honest with her. 'I really don't. I'd do it anyway.'

She smiles, surprised.

'We're going to work on our design for the logo and stuff, and draft some letters. We want to get funding for care centres and schools and places that work with disadvantaged kids. I can't stop thinking about Anna's daughter,

Lily. There's lots of things we can do to help people. Things that people might not even think of . . .'

Hah. If only she knew how many people we'd be helping if we can fix it.

'Okay,' she says. 'You can go. But only because I like Jake and Aaron.' She says this like she's saying *they'll be a good influence on you.*

'Thanks, Mum!' Then something snags at the back of my mind. 'Mum, how would you go about finding someone's distant relatives? You know, can you track them down somehow?'

She frowns. 'Yes, there are all kinds of ways you could do that. I could do it through work. We have associates of the firm who work with the Registry of Births and Deaths. Do you know the name?'

'Yeah. Frederick Mason. It's Aaron's dad – well, he died. But Aaron's looking for his relatives.'

'I'll see what I can do,' she promises, then stops me before I leave the room. 'Just . . . make sure you have some fun, too, okay?'

I grin, but inside I'm feeling guilty and nervous and, yeah, just a little bit scared.

***

In keeping with our ruse, I get Anna to drop me off at Jake's house. Nina makes pancakes for tea.

'They're my favourite!' Daniel says. 'Thanks, Nina.'

'I wish I could say that's why I made them,' Nina says grumpily. 'I've been craving pancakes all day. This kid –' she looks down at her stomach – 'is going to be the fattest baby in the world.'

It's really hard to think of a little person growing inside her, and it kind of grosses me out, so I concentrate on getting my mixture of maple syrup and chocolate syrup perfect.

'Oh, it just proves he's got good taste,' Mr Miles says, coming in from the lounge room. He half-hugs her then takes a seat. The table is crowded, with me, Jake, Daniel, Keira, and Aaron, and we all scrunch together to make room. I think of the dinner with my parents the other night – the awkwardness and space.

I think I know which one I prefer.

I'm so jealous of Jake.

'Nina showed me your design for a logo, Mikhal,' Mr Miles says. 'It's great. You know, I can run-off copies at the office if you need it. My secretary, Jen, orders colour cartridges for the multifunction copier, but we only ever use black and white for printing.'

'Thanks.' I'm still wondering why everyone thinks it's so great.

'I was talking to Jen on the phone earlier, and I mentioned this concert idea you had,' he goes on. 'There's a band called *Alter Ego* –'

'Alter Ego?' I drop my fork.

Mr Miles looks alarmed. 'Hm, well, I was talking to my secretary,' he says. 'And her brother plays the lead guitar –'

I look at Keira. Her mouth is hanging slightly open. She's knows them, too – of course she does. Everyone does. 'You mean – he's *in* Alter Ego? *The* Alter Ego – '*Starlight Flight*' Alter Ego?'

'I don't know,' Mr Miles says. 'I'm not exactly sure about rock singers –'

'They're not rock. They're post-punk alternative,' I can't help but interrupt him. You just can't get a detail like that wrong. 'And they're completely insane.'

'Oh,' Mr Miles says, sounding uncertain.

'That means "good",' Nina supplies. 'Insane is good. Am I right?'

'It means they're fantastic.' Keira says. 'They're all over YouTube.'

I can't even think. It's mind-blowing that Alter Ego might play in Cassidy Heights.

'But anyway,' Mr Miles continues, 'She told me they would be willing to do a charity show for a reasonable price.'

Instantly, I put my head in my hands. Of course. They've got an international name, now. They're not going to play a small town gig for free. 'How much?'

I'm afraid of the answer.

'She thought they'd probably do it for around a thousand dollars. They'd need to travel down here, and book accommodation.'

And there it is.

Nina smiles tightly. 'I don't think that'll work. We're not earning anything from the charity – it's costing us money to run. And we'd still have to pay for advertising.'

She's not saying it's costing *my mum* money to run.

'But it was nice of her to offer. Maybe if the Bridge Foundation takes off –' she smiles at me as she works the new name into the conversation. 'We can get someone smaller this time.'

But that's the thing. We could bring in tonnes if we had someone like Alter Ego. 'They won't take payment after the concert?' I ask desperately.

'They might agree to it,' Nina says. 'But we couldn't do that. It'd put us in a really bad position if we couldn't cover their costs. It wouldn't be fair to them.'

We're all pretty quiet after that.

***

We actually do play some games when we get to Mrs Henders place. She's acquired Jake's and Daniel's old Xbox since Aaron decided to stay with her, but we play cards instead, trying to put off what's coming next. We're all nervous. You can feel it.

Mrs Henders makes chamomile tea (for Keira and Jake and Aaron) and cocoa for me and

Daniel, and she puts a plate of homemade biscuits on the coffee table.

'This is an interesting idea,' she says. 'The significance of music is one that is well-noted by the Guardians. They devoted much time to the study of it and it's effects on the Ether. Whatever they discovered, the results were hidden. I think they were afraid of what they found.'

I'm wary of Mrs Henders. I didn't know either of my grandparents, and I've never spent much time around old people. She seems . . . fierce. I have a feeling she knows a lot about a lot of things, and that's why she's always listening so intently and scrutinising everyone.

Keira has explained her story to me. She told me everything – how Mrs Henders was born in Shar, and exiled for the crime of making the telescope that could show the bridges between the worlds. To make something like that, would have taken a lot of knowledge – and a lot of guts.

I can't quite see that person in the woman sitting there sipping tea out of a porcelain cup with roses on the sides.

'But we can't be sure it'll work,' Keira says. She's toying with her crystal, pressing the sides of it, tracing the tip over her palm.

'We've got to try.'

'If this works,' Mrs Henders says slowly, turning her gaze on Aaron, 'You may be able to go home. Have you thought about that?'

'I haven't thought about anything else,' Aaron says softly.

Keira looks up with a jerk. There's something in her expression that tells me *she* hasn't thought about this, even if Aaron has. Or maybe she was trying not to. 'We have to see,' she says resolutely. 'Mikhal? Did you bring your guitar? It's nearly eleven o'clock.'

Obviously I bought my guitar – the big zip-up case is sitting in the corner. My stomach flip-flops.

I can't do it. It's all wrong. I'm going to fail again.

Jake has his phone, and he plugs it into the power point using the charger I found in my drawer. He sits it in the middle of the floor.

'The lights were off,' I say. 'Maybe we should turn them off this time as well.'

I feel better in the darkness. There is light coming in through the window from the street-lights outside, but at least now they can't see my face.

'Okay,' Keira says, when we're all seated in a ring on the floor, except for Mrs Henders, who remains in her chair.

'I feel like we're holding a séance,' Mrs Henders says with a laugh, then covers her mouth. 'Oh. I can't believe I said that.'

'Okay,' Keira says, her voice urging me to hurry. Her crystal dances through her fingers. 'That's good . . .'

It's not good, and I know it.

But I have to do this.

I open my mouth, and the words spill out.

'I'm sorry, sorry, sorry –
There's a thousand words,
But none of them justify
Clarify
Nullify . . .'

I start to hum wordlessly. It doesn't matter about words or chords. There are no semiquavers, or music staves in this song. It's all about the sound.

'wiiisshhhoo . . .'

The words elongate and crackle.

'. . . wish you could hear me . . .'

'Cari?' Jake says, tentatively. 'Cari – is that you?'

Some small sound, a surprised little gasp, then a laugh. 'Jake? Jake? *Jake?*'

'Yeah, yeah!' Jake babbles quickly. 'It's me! Cari, it's me. I'm here.'

'I'm so glad to hear your voice. I've been –'

'Where are you?'

There is a pause. 'I don't know. I don't know exactly. It's a place between. There is nothing above me, and only the rushing of the silver waters around me. I think I'm in the Ether. Inside it. It's like being inside a... a bowl, perhaps, with water running over the edges, swirling through a hole in the bottom. The sides are so smooth. I've tried climbing, but I just slip back down – the waters push me back to the bottom, and twice now I've almost fallen into the hole where the water swirls.' A tremor in her voice makes is sound thinner. 'There is a thread that reaches from the device – your phone. It stretches across the bowl. One end vibrates with your world, Jake, and the other rests in Shar. Just like when I first spied on your world, only now, I can see the things that are happening in both worlds.'

'Are you okay?' Jake's voice is strained. 'It's been two weeks. Cari – you've had nothing to eat or drink in all that time –'

'But you left me only hours ago,' Cari replies.

'Time must move differently in the place between.' It's Aaron who says this, the first one of us who dares to interrupt Jake's moment with Cari.

Keira is nodding. 'Only a few minutes had passed when I arrived back from Shar.'

But Cari is focused on something else. 'Archon?' she says.

'It is me.'

'Archon, I'm glad to hear you. I have seen your mother, and your sister. They are well. They have been taken into the Guardians' protection.'

'Protection?' Aaron gasps. 'They've been imprisoned?'

'The Guardians are no longer using the prison chambers beneath the Citadel. Your escape has rendered it useless. They are being kept under watch instead, and they've been questioned thoroughly. But they have not been harmed.'

'We don't have much time left,' Keira hisses. 'Cari, we've managed to make some kind of bridge using music. But we don't know how long this will last.'

'I can hear the music. It sounds wonderful, and I think it's having an effect on the thread of gold reaching out from the . . . the phone,' she says. 'It's much stronger now. I can almost hold it.'

'Can you use it to draw yourself through?'

'I could try. But it's – tenuous. I can feel the wavering vibrations. If it broke, I think the waters would sweep me away. I might be lost forever.'

'Don't!' Jake yelps, then continues more quietly. 'Don't try it. I don't . . . you shouldn't . . . risk it.'

Everyone can hear what he's not saying. *I don't want to risk losing you.*

I'm amazed, then, at how much he obviously feels for her. I didn't really think people our age could fall in love. But I don't think there's any other word to explain what is in Jake's expression and his voice.

I look over at Keira, her hand gripping Aaron's knee. Are they? Is it . . . is it like that for them, too? I'm a bit jealous.

I'm still singing and playing and realise that the music is doing this – that I'm doing this – making the connections between them visible. And stronger.

'What are we going to do?' Daniel says. It's

the first time he's spoken. 'Is there any way we can bring you home, Cari?'

'Home?' Cari gives a little laugh. 'I'm not sure where that is, now! I'm not welcome in my world. I'm not part of yours. But that's not . . .' There is a burst of rushing noise. It's the river of noise that's trapping Cari – it's getting stronger. I hit a few louder, discordant notes, trying to drown it out. '. . . important right now. If the Guardians intend to destroy your world, we need . . . stop them.'

'We need your help to do that, Cari!' Daniel protests. His voice is shrill over the growing noise of the river.

And my song. I'm losing it. It's so hard to concentrate . . .

'It's true,' Jake says. 'We really need your help with this. You can draw threads between your world and this one, Cari. We're going to need you with us.'

Cari is silent. 'Then I have to try to break through . . . no other way.'

There's another eruption of noise. I can't help it. My fingers slip on the strings.

I have to ask this question. 'If there are other worlds out there – and there are thousands, aren't there? – why are the Guardians so concerned with this one? Why do they want to destroy us so badly?'

'Earth resonates very closely with Shar. Of all the worlds, yours poses the most danger to them.' Cari says sadly. 'Your world is a powerful place.' She sounds wistful, like she misses our world very much. 'I could just step through . . .' she says again.

'Cari, don't do anything.' I stop singing and yell this. 'Just wait. Don't do anything, okay? Just wait!'

It's too late. The river is too loud. I don't know whether she heard me or not, but she's gone now. The phone is dead.

'No.' Jake shakes his head disbelievingly, hopelessly.

'It's okay. We'll rescue her. We'll figure out a way.' Keira says. 'We *will*. Somehow.'

'How? We don't even have the telescope!'

'When you were talking to Cari, I could see these . . . things. These connections. She talked about threads, and I think that's what they were – maybe it's something to do with the Ether or whatever you call it.' I'm babbling, trying to get this all out. 'And I'm wondering – if the music makes them visible, and stronger – what would happen if I could make them strong enough to make a bridge? Cari could cross over.'

They're all staring at me and I wonder if I've just said something so completely stupid . . .

'That's it,' Keira says. 'That's exactly it. We just need to figure out how to do it.'

'The Ether can be worked,' Mrs Henders says. 'You know this, girl. What have you been practising?'

Keira cocks her head to one side, thinking. The crystal shard is in her hands, glinting with a thousand colours. 'Yes. But can – am I strong enough to do this? I mean, I'm not a Guardian. And if what Cari has seen is true, they'll do everything they can to stop us.'

'I would suggest you sleep on it,' Mrs Henders says. 'I do not need your parents blaming me when you fall asleep in your classes tomorrow.'

Even though this sounds like good advice, and we all lie down in our sleeping bags and close our eyes, I don't think any of us actually sleep that night.

Chapter Six:
The Next Day

I DO a great impression of a zombie the next day at school. Everyone knows something's up.

Baz takes a seat next to me in Maths.

'What's up with you?'

'Sick,' I groan, and he backs away, holding his hands up and making a face. He takes the seat behind me instead, leaving the chair next to me for Sharna.

'Hey!' she says. 'I'll help you with this trigonometry stuff. It's *crazy* what you can do with trig.'

I try to contain my enthusiasm.

'You're falling asleep,' she complains, halfway through explaining that x and y are something-something.

'I had a late night.'

She huffs. 'If you're going to do well at school, you can't just go staying up all night. What were you doing, playing games?'

'Of course not,' I protest, but since I can't tell her I'm on a mission to save the world, it comes out sounding kind of lame. Then I wonder why

I care what she thinks. 'I just can't do this. It's so boring that by the time I've figured out the question I don't even care about the answer.'

'Well, maybe you should think about the practical applications of an equation like this,' she says. She continues. 'Like . . . wheels on a car. See, a tangent touches the wheel at one point exactly. If the wheel is perfectly circular and the road is perfectly straight . . .'

She sees my blank expression. I'm still sitting here trying to get over the fact that she used the words *practical applications* in a sentence.

She sighs. 'Well, how about this. If you need to walk from one point to another, you can use Pythagoras's Theorem to get there much more quickly.'

'Except that I can't walk over houses or buildings. So I'd still have to stick to the roads, and in Cassidy Heights, none of them were designed by Pythagoras.'

I wonder suddenly what colour she is. It's a strange thought and for a moment I can't think where it came from – then I remember, or remember remembering. It's what Keira showed me of the people in Shar. How they can see people's auras – the colour of their personality, the colour of their mood.

I have a feeling right now she'd be bruise-purple with anger and frustration. Her lips are pursed. 'You're just being obtuse. Deliberately. It's really annoying.'

I'm glad I've annoyed her. It makes her look – and sound – more human.

'So trigonometry is useless,' she continues, her cheeks getting pink as her anger rises. 'Every building in this city has been designed using it. All the furniture in those buildings. They reckon the Ancient Egyptians used it to build their pyramids. Astronomers were using trigonometry to calculate star positions ages ago. Your stupid PlayStation . . . I mean, it's all relevant.'

'All right, class, if you'll listen up for a moment,' Mr Holloway, the teacher says. 'We're having an impromptu test. Just answer as best you can,' he gives me a pointed look, but Sharna glances at me.

'You know this stuff,' she says. 'You can do it.'

I stare at the questions. Amazingly, some of them *do* make sense. But I'm still not sure I've got them right.

It's Andrew, though, who makes my bad day really crappy. Mrs Hilderbrand gave him the dreaded pink detention slip for fighting. To him, my punishment – enforced slavery to the Bridge Foundation – looks like I'm getting off scot-free.

So he decides to make my life hell.

He starts with my locker. Tipping lockers is year-seven stuff, but between every class, he does it to mine. And because there are three other lockers in my bank, all those people hate me too, once their books have crashed out onto the floor for the sixth time.

In Music, Andrew loosens all the strings on the guitar I always use – the only good one in the bunch of them. School guitars, unfortunately, don't get a good deal out of life, and Andrew just makes it worse. I know it was him, because he never touches the guitars – he thinks he's a legend on the drums – but he's hanging around by the rack where the guitars are lined up when I come in. I have to spend ten minutes tuning it back up.

Mr Jackson growls at us for wasting time. 'I know you two don't want be working together,' he says. 'But I'm not letting you off. Cooperation is something you have to learn, boys. I'll put you in the studio last, okay? See if you've managed to work out something harmonious between the two of you.'

Cassidy Heights High School got a grant to install a proper studio, with all this professional equipment. Some of it has been damaged or broken, of course, because there's always kids who just have to stick bubblegum in the wrong places or just wreck things because they can, but it's guarded obsessively by Mr Jackson. Most of it's still in good condition.

You enter through a smaller box-shaped control room, which I've always loved, because it's chock-full of cool looking stuff like slider boards, and computer monitors, and blinking lights. There's a long glass window showing the wedge-shaped recording area.

'You go in and set-up the drums and stuff. I'll fix things up in here,' Andrew says. 'Just shut the door so I can get the sound perfect.'

I shrug and go through the 'live room', shutting the door. I'm bending over to plug in the guitar when the speaker in front of my face bursts to life with an ear-shattering screech.

'Shit!' I yell and stumble backwards, only I don't hear myself because all I can hear is the resounding screech of feedback in my ears.

I can see Andrew through the window, laughing his head off.

Mr Jackson wrenches open the door to the control room and marches in. 'What's going on in here?'

'It was an accident,' Andrew protests, stifling his laughter. 'Someone set the dials up too high.'

Mr Jackson doesn't look like he quite believes Andrew's excuse, but he leans through the second door into the live room, asking if I'm all right.

He's a tall man, and I like him more than I've ever liked any other teacher. I actually look forward to music classes.

'You know, you're doing good work on this composition, Mikhal. I'm going to make sure Mrs Hildebrand knows that.'

I give a half-smile, maybe because I can only just barely make out what he's saying through the ringing in my ears.

'You're good with music. You should think about pursuing it professionally. You know, I can give you private lessons.'

'Thanks,' I say, adding the *but I'm not interested* silently. 'But I'm pretty busy. I'm organising this charity thing. I don't think I'd have time.'

He looks at me thoughtfully. 'I'll talk to you about this further, Mikhal. I don't like to see students wasting their talent.'

Andrew isn't finished yet.

During PE, he makes sure we're opposing teams for doubles tennis and serves his ball into my face about five hundred times. Then he accidentally loses the scoresheet out of the folder when he's taking it over to the teacher, and argues that he won by five points instead of just two. When the bell rings, he walks past the fence where I've dumped my bag, picks it up, and walks five metres to dump it in the mud.

I'm mad and sitting there, scraping mud off my bag when I hear them.

The magpies again. They're like storm clouds, like a tornado. They whirl around and around as they whip through the air. It's a pretty amazing sight.

I see Sharna standing not far away from me, her tennis racquet still in one hand, the other hand shielding her eyes.

'Something's wrong,' she says to no one in particular. 'There's just too many of them. Magpies flock, just like all birds do, but to see so many? There's not enough food for so many of them – and it's winter.'

I can't help but agree. Whatever's going on with those birds is weird.

And kind of creepy.

'There are mice in our house, too,' I say, remembering Anna screaming. 'We've never had mice before.'

'We need to work more on your essay,' she tells me as we walk back to school. 'It's due at the end of the week. Have you even started?'

'No,' I say. 'Well, I mean, I've *thought* about it.'

She rolls her eyes. 'Are you busy this evening?'

'Yes,' I say instinctively. I've got heaps to do. I need to figure out how to rescue Cari, and I don't have time for schoolwork. But Sharna's gaze is hard and sharp, and I start to feel guilty. 'No.'

I open my locker and find tomato sauce has been squeezed through the vents of my locker.

Yuck.

'Oh, gross,' Sharna says. She knows about my fight with Andrew – everyone does by now. 'It's kind of funny, you know. It's like a vendetta.'

I snort. 'You're the only person in the world who would use a word like that in real life.'

She looks at me thoughtfully. 'Is that a bad thing?'

'No. I didn't say that. It's just – unusual.'

Anna drives us home, and we dump our books on the coffee table in the living room. I automatically reach for the TV remote, but

Sharna shoots me a glare, and I guiltily put it back.

Mum pokes her head in. 'Mikhal, I've got a few names from the Registry,' she says, holding out a printed sheet. 'You know, possible relatives of your friend's father? There were a few Frederick Mason's listed, but only one of them was the right age and was listed as dead. I did a little digging, too – I hope your friend doesn't mind, but my associate was able to give me one of the addresses, and it's not too far from here. In Swan Lakes.'

'Oh, that's awesome,' I say, taking the list. There are five names – two women, three men. Three Mason's, one Townsend, one Lovell. There's no information on where they live, only dates that tell me they're still alive, and around the same age as my parents are. Were they brothers, sisters, cousins? I wonder about these people, who presumed that Frederick Mason went missing in their world. They would have spent weeks, months, hoping that he'd turn up before finally accepting that he was dead, that he wasn't ever coming back. Their lives went on. They had children of their own, probably. None of them would know the truth unless Aaron tells them.

I suddenly realise I've been using subtraction to work the dates out in my head, and I feel a twinge of amazement. Maybe this whole maths thing is working after all.

'Tell him I can take him out there if he likes

– there are a few things I need to pick up from a charity depot out that way. I'm free most of next week.'

'I'll ask him,' I promise, folding the piece of paper while Mum smiles over my head at Sharna.

'We're getting the exterminators in tomorrow afternoon,' she says. 'I found mouse droppings in my briefcase in court this morning.'

'You're going to kill them?' I say, momentarily horrified. Sharna looks green.

'Oh, no. Just have them trapped and removed. Apparently they've had heaps of calls – it was hard to get a booking. Not just them, the guy said; there've been cockroaches and spiders and even wasps flying around – would you believe it? Wasps in winter!'

'Wasps usually hibernate during winter,' Sharna says. 'They do shelter inside, in people's attics or roof spaces. But it's definitely unusual for them to be flying around during cold weather.'

'So how do you know so much about animals?' I ask her.

She shrugs. 'I just do. I like animals. I like anything to do with the environment.'

I've heard the usual greenie speech before, but Sharna's explanation is a bit different. She's not just going around telling people to recycle. She's interested in what's happening, too.

'Since humans have started pumping toxins

into the atmosphere, the rate of global warming has increased alarmingly. We're making more changes to the planet than any species ever has. We need to realise what we're doing and control it. But we're faced with corporations . . .'

She trails off, looks at me sideways. 'You're laughing at me, aren't you?'

'What? No.' I'm offended, because I really wasn't. I was actually interested in what she was saying. 'I'm just wondering. What happens if what we're doing to the world doesn't just affect this planet? What if it, like, goes right out into the universe? And upsets the balance of everything?'

She frowns. 'Well, it's not impossible.'

'I just think . . .' I'm thinking, of course, of the Ether and what I've learned about Shar, and the possibility of other worlds. 'That everything's kind of connected.'

'You're a lot smarter than you pretend to be!' Sharna exclaims, then she looks at me again, her eyes looking deep and sparkling with excitement.

I think that's about as close to a compliment as I'm ever going to get from Sharna.

Then, suddenly, she leans over and kisses me.

It's so quick I'm left wondering if it actually happened. My lips tingle where she touched them with her lips, but she doesn't look embarrassed or surprised or *anything*. She just grabs an exercise book and starts scribbling.

'So, you need to split your essay into three parts – an introduction comes first . . .'

We're interrupted by Mum, who smiles when she sees Sharna. 'Oh, you're working.'

'Don't look so surprised, Mum,' I roll my eyes.

'I'm just popping over to Georgia's place. We need to sort out a venue for this concert, if it's going to go ahead.'

'You know,' Sharna pipes up. 'If you're planning a concert, you could probably use the pagoda at the Phoenix Park. That way, it's outside so you don't have to worry about spilled drinks or food.'

'That's not a bad idea,' Mum says thoughtfully. 'Do you think we can get council permission?'

'I'm positive.'

Of course she can. Sharna can talk any adult into doing whatever she wants.

'Oh!' I suddenly remember. 'Mr Miles, Jake's dad, said he could get this really cool band to play. *Alter Ego.*'

'Those punk rockers on your poster?' she looks dubious.

'People would pay heaps to come and see them! But they're going to need payment up front.'

'Hm.' Mum frowns. 'I'm not sure . . .'

'Yeah,' I sigh. 'I know. It's just – I know we could cover the costs and raise heaps of money as well. People would travel to see them, you know. It really sucks.'

'Well,' Mum says, but she doesn't finish that sentence, just leaves the room.

'You're really into this charity stuff, aren't you?' Sharna says.

I shrug. 'I don't really know what I'm doing. I just want it to work.'

There's that look in her eyes again, and all of a sudden I want to kiss her again. 'Why did you do that?' I ask her.

'What?' she bites her lip, which is such an unsure expression for her that I know she knows exactly what I'm talking about.

'Kiss me.'

She gives a half-smile, and she is about to answer, when Mum strides back in from the kitchen. She's clutching one of her Visa cards, which she hands to me.

'I'm going to trust you with this,' she says. 'Find out how much the band will take to come and play. If it's less than two thousand dollars, you can get them to charge the card. Okay?'

'Really?' I gape at her.

'You've proved you can be responsible, Miky. Remember, we can't pay more than two thousand.'

'Yeah, yeah, okay!' I grin at her. I tuck the card into my wallet. Wow. Alter Ego, playing in Cassidy Heights? This is the most awesome thing ever!

'So, who is this Alter Ego?' Sharna asks.

I gape at her for a moment, then I shake my head and tell her to come with me.

In my room, I push some clothes off my bed so she can sit down. I hit 'play' on my stereo, and Alter Ego's latest single 'Dive' blasts out. Sharna covers her ears.

'Yowch!'

'Just listen to the melody,' I tell her. 'Listen to the bass. Most bands use bass guitar as backing and forget it can be used as an instrument. They really know what they're doing.'

She looks thoughtful. She's bought her notebook up with her, and she kneels on the floor so she can lean on the bed and scribble over all the work we've done so far. 'Forget this. You're going to do your essay on music.'

'What? Why?'

'Because,' she explains, 'clearly, you care about this. Believe me, you'll be able to write the most amazing essay if you can really care about what you're writing. And, see, you can apply this to your maths, too. Music is multiple frequencies that enter your ear at the same time, and you can use sine waves to work out why some combinations of those frequencies are more pleasing to hear than others . . .'

'Can you stop that for a moment?' I tell her, annoyed. 'Just put the book down for a second.'

She hears the disapproval in my tone and looks puzzled. 'Okay,' she says, putting the pen down.

I grab her arm and pull her to her feet.

'Now just . . . close your eyes and listen. Don't *think* about anything.'

'Okay,' she agrees. And we stand there for a moment, letting the pounding music echo in our ears. I know she feels it. I can tell she sees it the way I do.

'You can dance, can't you? I saw you dancing with Jake at my party.'

She laughs, but doesn't open her eyes. 'Yeah. I took lessons until I was about twelve.'

'Why did you stop?'

She shrugs and frowns. 'I . . . I don't know. I kind of got wrapped up in other things. School . . .'

'Why do you care so much about school?'

'Because it's something I'm good at. I can do it really well, if I try.'

I can't quite get my head around this. Why spend so much of your time and energy on something like school? Why care so much about your grades? But I can tell it really is important to her. She's not just saying it – she feels it.

Her voice is quiet as she continues. 'There are a lot of things I want to do in life. To do them, I need to get good grades and get into a good university.'

'What do you want to do?'

'Marine biology.'

I laugh, suddenly. I can't help it, remembering the conversation with Anna about her daughter, Lily, and how every girl wants to be a marine biologist at one point in her life. Her eyes fly open and she glares at me. 'Why is that funny?'

'I wasn't laughing at you,' I amend.

'No. Just *about* me, right? Just because you don't care, Mikhal, doesn't mean the rest of us are willing to just sit back and do nothing!' She's shouting, and I'm a bit alarmed.

The music echoes loudly in my ears, but it sounds different now. The magic of the moment is gone. She marches out of the room.

***

I know I should have chased her, apologised, and tried to make it better. But I can't bring myself to move. She hates me – she's always hated me, just a little bit. And why should I apologise? She's the one who takes everything so personally.

What's her problem, anyway? All this stuff about school and succeeding – can't she just have fun for a while?

Sharna left her exercise book on the bed. I flick through it. Her writing is neat and even, like she's typed it. I stop on the page with the maths stuff.

How can this make sense to anyone?

It's like it's in another language. She hasn't just copied down the things the teacher put up on the whiteboard, like the rest of us. She's scribbled things on top of other things, trying to get everything down as Mr Holloway talked. There are lines and graphs and x's and y's all over the place.

I shake my head, but something about it seems . . . hm. What is it *about*? I'm surprised that I care, but something about it catches my interest.

Increasing and decreasing.

The little wavy lines seem like sound waves. Up and down, the way they look on a computer screen when you're recording. Maybe this stuff *does* have a use in the real world. You could work out how much sound you were producing, and how to increase it. You could figure out how to blow out someone's eardrums . . .

I grab the phone and call Jake.

'What if sound waves could do more than just break through the boundary?'

'What are you talking about?' he asks.

'Well, I'm just thinking. Sound waves disturb the air. But if it's true that they can also make connections, if they were strong enough, they could maybe make a solid bridge. What do you think?'

Jake gives a little sound, a 'huh.' I can't tell if he's impressed, but I can tell he's thinking.

'I'm almost sure this will work,' I go on. 'At least, it's worth a try.'

'We'd need to test it. But I don't know exactly how that would work. I mean, your song got through to Cari, but we can't risk her getting swept away in the Ether.'

'I was just playing acoustic. It wasn't exactly very loud, meaning the vibrations weren't all that strong. But if it was louder, more focused, maybe it would work.'

Jake sounds excited, but I think he's holding his enthusiasm back. 'How do we make it loud enough?'

That's a good question.

***

I write a song that night, once the exterminators have gone.

The words spill out of me. All I can think of is Sharna.

'How can you drive me so insane?
When I'm around you I can't
Remember my own name –
You're reaching for something impossible
A dream is just a dream because you'll
always wake
Can't you see how much you frustrate me?
Making me feel like I can only fail
But you're the one who'll disappoint me'

A mouse runs across my bed, startling me. Guess they didn't get them all. It stops and looks at me with tiny little beady eyes.

'What do you think?' I ask it.

It twitches its whiskers and darts away.

I stare at the words on the page. Even if the mouse doesn't think much of them, I know they're perfect. They're everything she makes me feel – confused, like I want to do more, be more than I am – but how can I possibly be anything different?

Do I even want to be?

Chapter Seven:
The Wall

THE next day, Mr Holloway passes back our tests. With a nod to me, he says 'Good work, Mikhal.'

I glance at Sharna, who is yet again sitting next to me. I'm expecting her to be as excited as I am, but all she says is: 'You got a B. That's great.'

'Oh, okay.'

'So, we should probably start working on the hypotenuse now...'

I pull out the exercise book she left in my bedroom and put it on the table. It succeeds in shutting her up, but then she just sits there staring glumly at it.

'That stuff about increasing and decreasing,' I say. 'I'm just wondering. How would you work out how much you need to increase a number, in order for it to reach a certain level?'

Just as I suspected, she can't resist working out this problem. 'Well, you'd need to know what value you need to reach. You'd start with your initial amount and . . . what *exactly* are we talking about, here?'

'Sound waves,' I explain. 'I have a particular tone. I need to increase it by certain amounts until I reach a level where it . . . well, I'm not sure what will happen. But I'll know when it gets there.'

'Oh, right,' she says thoughtfully. 'Well, look at it this way.'

She starts to scribble on a page.

'Do you know what frequency is?'

I shake my head. She pulls her exercise book closer to her and draws a wavy line.

'Frequency is the number of waves that pass a fixed place in a certain amount of time. They're measured in a unit called hertz.'

She draws a wavy line on the page. The vertical lines are close together, connected by shallow curves.

'This is a high frequency wave,' she says.

She draws another one, and labels it 'low frequency.' On this one, the lines are gentler, more spaced out.

'So if a certain note – like an **"A"** note played on a violin – vibrates a certain number of times a second at the same speed, or similar, we recognise that as 'pitch'. If we assume that they can repeat at the same oscillation for a period of time, we can measure the rate of repetition, which is what we call frequency.'

'Right,' I say, then pause. 'I'm completely lost.'

'If you know what frequency your instrument, or the note you're playing, is resonating at, you can probably work out which combinations of notes are most likely to reach the hertz you need using a mathematical formula. I can help you, if you like.'

She's right, I suddenly realise. She's the perfect person to help, and not just with the maths side of things.

***

When I meet the others at lunch time, I'm dragging Sharna behind me. 'We have to talk about saving Cari,' I say.

Keira eyes Sharna, and does not look happy. 'Miky, what are you doing?'

I take a deep breath. 'We need Sharna to help us.'

Sharna looks mystified.

'She knows about frequencies. And she's got access to the front office, which is what we need right now. Besides, we can trust her.'

Keira looks dubious. 'With everything?'

'Yes,' I say, looking back at Sharna. 'Can't we?'

She looks unsure. 'I . . . I guess. It's nothing . . . bad, is it? You're not breaking the law?'

'Hah!' Keira laughs, Jake chuckles, and Aaron smiles.

'Not yet,' I say. 'Aaron? Can you use the . . . whatever it is . . . like Keira did with me?'

'The *ihlwarh* isn't supposed to work on most humans,' Keira says.

'I have a feeling that it works on those people it's meant to work on. It is a part of the Ether, and the Ether seems to have worked to bring us together.' Aaron says this in his usual serious tone. 'I was able to see into Sharna's mind once before. I take that as a sign.'

He's talking about at the reception desk, the first time I saw him. How he knew Sharna had put the papers in the drawer. If only I'd known, back then, that he was reading her mind!

'The Ether is all about connections, isn't it?' I add. 'I think those connections were working even before I knew anything about this.'

'Would someone please tell me what's going on?' Sharna says in a small voice. 'You're making me nervous.'

Aaron nods. 'I can show you.'

And then Aaron touches her. I watch her face as the *ihlwarh* washes over her, the slow dawning realisation, the stunned amazement, the absolute wonder. I guess I must have looked like that when Aaron did it to me.

She opens her eyes and looks right at me.

I can't help looking at her lips.

'Is this true?' she asks.

'Yeah,' I say. 'It is.'

***

As the others head inside, I tug on Aaron's arm, getting him to hang back with me. I give Aaron the list of Frederick Mason's relatives. He looks at it helplessly.

'But your world is so big,' he says. 'How will I ever find them?'

I shrug, feeling bad, like I've dangled a carrot in front of a caged rabbit. 'My mum's offered to drive you to one of the addresses, if you like. You can try and look up the phone number and call first, or I can come with you...'

'You'd do that?' Aaron's eyes widen.

'Yeah, of course!' I say. 'We could go on Saturday, if you want.'

He folds the paper and tucks it into his pocket. 'Yes,' he says. 'Thank you.'

***

The birds are on the news that night.

'. . . besieged by flocks of magpies. Recently, there have also been reports of unprecedented numbers of sparrows, swans, ducks and even seagulls being spotted in the area . . .'

The newsreader looks mildly amused, but when they show the footage, it's like something out of that Hitchcock movie. There are hundreds of thousands of birds. What is going on?

At least I have good news for Mum, though. I give her my maths test.

'You got a B?' she says. 'Oh, Mikhal! That's

wonderful!'

I have to tell Mum I'm tired from all my studying so she won't think it's suspicious that I'm going to bed at ten o'clock. I don't sleep. I'm lying there, completely tense, until my alarm goes off at ten to eleven.

I didn't change out of my clothes, so all I have to do is pull on my runners. I take the back staircase so that if Dad's in his study he won't hear me going through the front hallway. I use the back door. It's surprisingly easy. I've never really bothered to sneak out before – I've never had a reason to. But now, with everything about school, I figure it's probably best they think I'm still being the model child.

I'd stashed my bike outside the garage earlier in preparation, and I think Anna would be proud that I'm riding it. My breath makes little puffs of steam in the night air.

It's *freezing*.

But the birds don't seem to mind.

They're perched on the fences and in the trees and on the power lines. Some of them are singing. Some of them are fighting, flurries of feathers and claws and beaks. They're all restless, heads darting, wings fluttering, shifting from foot to foot.

I think they're watching me.

***

We meet at the gate outside the school. It's nearly half past eleven. Jake, Daniel and Aaron are already there – they live closest to the school. Keira arrives just after I do, her cheeks red from running in the cold wind.

'What's with all these birds?' she asks. 'They're freaking me out.'

'Is she going to come?' asks Jake anxiously. 'She might chicken out.'

I'm hoping she won't. But I have to admit, it's a possibility. It's already a few minutes late, and I remember that Sharna had gone pale at my suggestion of sneaking out.

'Have your parents ever told you you're not allowed to sneak out?' I asked her.

'Well, no. Dad just knows that I won't.'

'Then you're not disobeying him,' I coax. 'Right?'

She rolled her eyes. But there was something she wasn't telling me. I could see the tension in her shoulders and the worry in her eyes.

But then I'd asked her if she believed me.

'I don't know what to believe,' she said. 'This is kind of insane. More than insane.'

I know what she means, of course, but I just hope she won't let her sensible follow-the-rules side take over tonight. If she doesn't show up... this is all for nothing.

And, as if I've wished her into being here, there she is, walking quickly down the street, looking back over her shoulders as if she's expecting to be followed.

'Hey, you came!' I call.

'You sound surprised.' She sounds insulted.

'I didn't know if you would –'

'If I would have the guts?' Her eyes flash. 'Well, here's some news, Mikhal. I had to sneak past my dad, who was asleep on the couch! He almost woke up and caught me. I spent five minutes hiding behind the hallway door!'

I force down the urge to laugh, because something in her tone says that if he caught her it would be the worst thing that ever happened to her.

Really. She's way too uptight.

'No,' I say lightly. 'I'm glad you're actually here.'

I flash her a winning smile, and suddenly the tension is gone. She smiles back, and it lights up her face in the dull illumination flooding from the basketball court. I hoist myself up to the top of the fence and hold my hand down for her, but she ignores me and climbs the fence on her own. The others follow without any issues.

The soccer field seems enormous, and it takes forever for us to cross it. We stick to the shadows and walk quietly, but there are so many of us we can't help but make noise. And I keep getting the stupid urge to laugh.

We climb the low fence on the other side of the field. There are a few crows perched in the trees on the other side, and it feels like they're watching us – but maybe that's just my paranoia.

We're at the bike shed, which is built into the side of the gym, and we run quickly to the end, gathering in a huddle near the door.

We all look at Sharna. This is her job, now.

She looks nervous as she fishes in her pocket, pulling out the silver keyring I saw her holding in the office last week. Was it really only a few days ago? It feels like a lifetime!

I wonder how she managed to get them out of the office without anyone noticing.

'I'm not sure which one's which,' she whispers. 'My fingers are so cold!'

She tries one key, then another. The third one sticks, then, amazingly, turns smoothly. The door opens.

'Are you sure there isn't an alarm?' asks Keira.

'No, there is an alarm. But it won't go off if you use a key to enter,' Sharna explains patiently. She's told us all this before, but I think Keira wants reassurance. I think we all do. 'Same with the security cameras. No one will watch the footage unless they've got a reason to. Just don't go smashing any windows or anything, okay?'

Schools are not places you want to be at night. They look totally different when they're not full of students and teachers – and they sound different too. They're meant to be crowded and noisy. When they're empty, it's like they're full of ghosts.

I try not to let my uneasiness show on my face as we walk down the long corridor. Jake and Daniel have torches – we decided it would be better not to turn on any of the main lights in case someone notices – and they flick them on and off every now and then, just so we don't go falling over rubbish bins.

The stairwell at the end of the corridor leads us up to the music wing. Music rooms lead off to either side. We head for the room on the end, which is the music room that's used most of all, since it's the biggest and leads into the recording room. As we enter, I take my favourite guitar from the rack. It's got something sticky on the fretboard – some gross little Year 7's been using it, I think with an inward groan.

I lead the way into the control room, and look through the long glass window showing the wedge-shaped recording area. The walls and ceiling are covered in carpet, which is great insulation, especially when you're sneaking into a place you're not supposed to be in, planning on making a lot of noise.

Which is great.

'Okay,' I say, flicking on the computers and listening to the answering hum. 'I'll turn on all the speakers in the live room.' I point to the room beyond the window to show them what I mean. The lights are flickering on – it's okay to have them on in here, as there's no exterior windows. 'The amplified sound will be completely pure. And the insulation in the walls means it won't dissipate the way it does in a normal room . . .'

'Spare us the technical details, Mikhal,' Keira says dryly. 'Do I need to remind you we need to get out of here as quickly as possible?'

I make a face at her while I make a few of the adjustments I need to on the mixer board. Sharna stands at my shoulder, looking pale and ghost-like.

'Do you think this will work?' she asks.

'I don't know,' I reply. 'I really, really hope so.'

She nods, unhappily.

'Hey, don't worry. I promise you nothing bad will happen.'

She doesn't look like she believes me. I kind of want to kiss her again, make her forget about whatever she's worrying about – but we don't have time to even think about this.

'Come on,' I say, sitting down at one of the computers to show her how the program works. 'Everything that comes through the mixer will show up on the screen. These are the channel equalisers. You can boost the frequency by moving the slider up and down. You can muck around on the mixer board, too, to get it at the right level, okay?'

'Um, yeah, I think so,' she replies.

'The mic will be turned on both ways, so I can hear you and you can hear me,' I tell them before heading through into the live room.

The others are taking seats on the chairs in the control room, setting the phone on a blank space between the buttons and dials of the mixer board so they can all see it. Sharna looks up at me through the glass panel that separates the control room from the live room as I plug the guitar in with a crackle of feedback. I turn the dials on the amplifier until it clears, then pluck a few notes and tune the strings until they're pitch-perfect.

'Right – are you ready?' Keira says. 'Just play what you played the other night.'

I take a deep breath. I remember what I'd told to Sharna – don't think about it, just listen to the music.

It's easier to dish it out than it is to take it.
Don't think about it. Just play.
So I do.

> *'I told you*
> *I told you I'd wait, and I meant it'*

The sound wells up around me, trapped by the walls, resounding in our ears. It fills the room like smoke. You can breathe it in, feel it in your lungs. I watch Sharna, looking intently at the computer screen. She's nodding. I'm on the right track.

> *'I'd give you all you want*
> *I'll watch you*
> *I'll watch for you*
> *Don't want to be alone, don't want to be*
> *lonely, don't want to be alone . . .'*

I don't look at any of the others, though I can see them clearly through the window. Daniel, excitement written all over his young face. Aaron, looking hopeful and grave at the same time. Jake, looking like he's burning with something deep inside that he can't quite manage to let out. Keira, unable to sit still, her hands fluttering in her lap.

Sharna, looking at me in amazement, as if she never knew it was possible I could do this.

I concentrate on completing the connections, on the sounds I'm making.

'Cari?' Jake says.

'. . . Jake? Oh, I'm so glad . . .'

It's connected. *Yes!*

'Cari, we're going to try and make a bridge to you. Can you see anything? Can you try and use the thread to pull yourself through?'

'. . . can't hear you . . .'

I look at Sharna. She leans over, moves one of the sliders on the mixer board, then moves it back. The numbers on her screen are jumping up and down. Her eyes are wide with amazement. I love that look on her – it means she's seeing more, she seeing what I'm seeing, she's looking beyond her whole practical 'this is the way it is' attitude.

We can see it now, even more than before. Not smoke – no, it's more like *mist*, curling and curving up the walls, making its way from the live room into the control room even through the padded door, growing thicker and thicker until it's like water.

'Jake? Are you there? Keira – Archon – are you there?'

Cari's voice comes through clearly now. I can see it through the window. There's a golden thread, thin as a strand of spider-web, stretching from the phone right up through the ceiling.

'Wow, can you *see* that?' Daniel says.

'Cari! We can see the thread. Can you reach it? Is it strong enough?'

'I can see it, Jake. I can see you. All of you.'

She's smiling – I can hear it in her voice, even through the speakers. But I can hear desperation underneath that.

'I can see the Guardians, too, Jake. It's bad. They . . . they have devised some plan. I can't be sure. But it's very near to completion. They speak of a wall that will divide our worlds, permanently.'

I don't have to remember to continue to play. My fingers find the notes without guidance. The song is almost playing itself, now – like something else is pulling the sounds from the guitar.

'A wall?'

Aaron interjects. 'There's already a boundary between the worlds. I don't know what they can mean by a wall.'

'A boundary isn't the same thing as a wall,' Sharna speaks softly.

'Yeah! A boundary isn't solid. It's just like... a line on a map, or some place you're not allowed through. But a wall is.' Daniel puts in. Dammit, that kid is smarter than I am.

'I have . . . I have seen my mother,' Cari continues. 'As well as some of the people she works with. And I'm so afraid . . . that her fear . . . Jake, when I was exiled, she was devastated. She blames your world for my doing what I did, for my disobedience, for my being imprisoned . . . she is doing everything she can to ensure the Guardians will succeed. Her fear gives her strength.'

There is deep emotion in her voice. She's beyond tears.

'If they succeed, Jake, you know what this will mean. Your world will be in terrible danger. The balance will be tipped. Your world... it will die.'

Her words chill me. 'What do you mean, die?'

'The balance will be tilted too far. It will no longer be connected by the *vinarhi*. No world can exist if it is cut off... Not for long, anyway.'

'Cari,' Jake says. 'Is the thread strong enough? Can you use it to pull yourself through?'

'I'm trying,' she says. 'But . . .'

Her voice fades away suddenly. The mist in the room is so thick I can hardly see anyone else. It glows with silver light. I can feel it cold on my cheeks. It's like water, but it's not wet. It's beautiful.

I can just see the others through the white fog, through the reflection on the window.

Sharna has stood up from her computer and is bending over the back of Daniel's chair. She says 'I can see something . . .'

She reaches out a hand, almost touching the golden thread that's leading upwards from the phone.

And then her head snaps around.

'Guys!' she yelps. 'Someone's coming!'

'Are you sure?' Keira asks. 'I didn't hear –'

Sharna stands up. She creeps across the control room to open the door slightly. The silver mist starts to dissipate. We all hear it then. A loud, echoing bang – the exact sound the weighted school doors make when they swing closed. Only without the usual noise of the crowds to absorb it, it sounds ominous. It's followed by the definite sound of movement and voices.

'Oh, crap!' I'm not sure who says it. Maybe it's me, but it doesn't sound like me. It sounds like it's coming from very far away. Everything that happens next happens in slow motion.

'Okay,' Sharna hisses, her voice surprisingly calm. 'Mikhal, you'll need to put the guitar back. Wait – unplug the cords first–'

I've almost dashed out of the live room with the guitar strap still slung around my neck, the leads still plugged into the amplifier. I quickly lift it over my head and pull out the cords, coiling them and sitting them back on top of the amp. Sharna opens the door for me, whispering to Jake to shut down the computers.

We listen to her. You can't help but listen to her.

The golden thread grows pale and starts to dissipate. The white mist is fading, too.

'Cari,' Jake says into the phone, whispering. 'I don't know if you can hear me. Just... hold on, okay? Hold on.'

He wraps the phone up with the charger. Someone turns off the lights.

The silver mist is only a few lingering traces near the ceiling, and even those are fading as I watch. Then I quickly hit the power buttons on the computers, holding them in so I don't have to waste time doing a proper shut down. This puts me behind everyone else . . . and I'm not sure this is where I want to be. It makes me itchy and impatient. No one's moving fast enough.

We hurry back through the music room, but when I pause to put the guitar back, I hit the edge of the rack. The guitar lets out a small thump, and the strings vibrate, carrying the sound on. I press a hand over the fretboard, stifling the sound. We all pause, waiting, wondering if whoever it was has heard us. There are more sounds of people talking, and footsteps.

The echo could be making them sound closer than they are. If they knew we were up here, surely they'd be here by now. They must be searching the corridor, room by room. Blood pounds in my ears.

By unspoken agreement we head for the same stairwell we came up. It's the closest one to the door by the gym, and we need to get outside as soon as we can.

The door to the stairwell is heavy. Since I'm the last one through I hold it and let it close slowly, then turn the handle so it won't make a noise as it clicks shut. I'm totally channelling James Bond right now!

Our shoes make slapping sounds on the tiles. One flight, whirl around the landing, another flight. We're nearly there! But the door at the bottom of the stairwell blocks our view of the corridor. What if they're out there?

To my amazement, it's Sharna who steps forward. She turns the handle very slowly, then eases the door open just a centimetre at first. The corridor is completely dark.

We breathe a collective sigh of relief, then, one by one, walk briskly out into the corridor. I'm left to shut the door, again. But – dammit – my hands are slippery with sweat by now – and I can feel it happening before it happens. My hand slips. The door bangs shut.

We all freeze, turning to look back at the door as if glaring at it will help. But only for a moment.

'Run!' hisses Sharna.

We bolt down the corridor. Our footsteps are echoing from the floor and ceiling, but there's no time to think about it. We fling ourselves through the open door at the end, bursting out into the cold night air and gasping.

Sharna shoves her way past me. I wonder what she's doing, but then I realise – she's re-locking the door behind us. It's a brilliant idea. How can she even think of things like that right now?

'Go!' she urges us.

We can see the lights are on in the music wing above and to our right. I tell myself that to anyone looking out, we'd only be shadows – and I doubt they'll be looking outside, anyway, with possible intruders *inside* the building. But it doesn't matter, because the air is full of birds.

There are even more of them now than there were. They seem to have been drawn to the school. They're all spiralling up, whizzing past the windows, perching on the gutters. And even though it's a scary sight, I'm grateful, because there's no way anyone will notice us moving through this flapping and shrieking crowd.

We pelt across the soccer field. The grass crackles with ice; how can the birds stand to be out in this cold? It's definitely not right. The freezing air burns my lungs, but there's no question about stopping. I look to my right and I can see cars have pulled into the parking lot. There's one car parked already, it's headlights on. I recognise it as Mr Jackson's car.

But there are other cars pulling in – with red and blue lights flashing on their roofs. Crap! The police! This is serious.

But what is Mr Jackson doing here? Did the police call him? Surely they wouldn't call him first-off – Mrs Hildebrand, maybe, but not the music teacher. Maybe it's the other way around, and he was here working late, and saw us creeping around the music wing, and called them.

But that's crazy, too. There weren't any lights on when we arrived. Unless he was working in the dark . . .

If we needed an incentive to keep going as fast as we can, the sight of those police cars is it. We reach the other side of the field in no time flat and jump the fence.

Even then, we run for another couple of blocks before we dare to stop.

'Keep walking,' Sharna says. 'If the police are out, they'll probably search the streets.'

Again, I'm amazed at her clear-headedness.

'We need to split up and get home.' Keira agrees.

Jake is clutching his phone, and I can see he almost has tears in his eyes. Keira grasps his arm. 'Hey, we'll try again. I swear, we'll figure this out. We'll talk about it tomorrow.'

Chapter Eight:
Higher Frequencies

JAKE, Daniel and Aaron head off together. Keira vanishes in the other direction. I know we need to hurry, but I can't help pinching the elbow of Sharna's jacket to hold her back for a moment. 'How did you do that? Keep your head? Geez. We never would have gotten out of there if you hadn't . . .'

She jerks away from me, her eyes flickering with anger.

'Don't!' she says. 'This was a stupid mistake. I can't believe we did that – that *I* –'

She chokes on a sob, then turns and starts to walk.

I start to go after her, but she's walking fast, and a car passes us, the headlights washing over the footpath, and I see that Sharna has vanished.

I duck my head and run for home.

***

I get a text from Keira at eight o'clock the next morning. '*Meet at the gate.*'

She's chosen the gate, of course, so that Daniel can join us before we go into school. We all look tired and worn out when we reach it.

'Where's Sharna?' I ask, but Keira shrugs. 'I sent her the text.'

I see her a half-second later, walking quickly across the parking lot with her head down. I wave to her, but she keeps walking. She can't have not seen us, and, besides, Keira sent her the text, too.

She's ignoring us. Or maybe just me.

'Okay,' Keira says. 'So, that didn't work.'

'Obviously.' Jake sounds bitter. I can tell he hasn't slept at all.

'I don't think it would have worked anyway,' I say. 'The sound wasn't right.'

'I think I know what you mean,' Aaron says. 'There was too much containment.'

'The walls of the live room are designed to trap sound and funnel it into the computers,' I say. 'And if you think about building a *real* bridge, well, the music – the song – can't be focused inwards, right? It needs to project outwards in order to make the connection.'

'Oh,' Keira says. 'So, how can we do that?'

'We could get all our stereos and hook them up together!' Daniel says.

Jake snorts.

'Actually, that's not such a bad idea,' I say.

'I mean, we could use some high-voltage

amplification equipment.' I grin at their blank faces. 'Big speakers. Really *big* speakers.'

'Really?' Daniel says, clearly impressed with himself. 'There's a music store in the mall.'

'Huh,' I say. 'The manager . . . doesn't like me.'

Even after Mum bought Roger for me I still get dirty looks from the storeowner, Ron, every time I go in there. He doesn't like me because I'm always looking at stuff and playing the guitars.'

'He doesn't like kids. We can't go there by ourselves.'

'You can call Mrs Henders!' Keira says to Aaron. 'She'll take us, won't she? Get her to meet us after school.'

Aaron agrees. 'She won't mind. I told her all about last night, and she was very sorry that it didn't work.'

It's weird to think of an adult being okay with us breaking into the school, but she's the only adult who knows – and believes – what's really going on, so I guess that makes all the difference.

***

I'm nervous when Sharna sits down next to me in Maths. But just like yesterday, once the teacher leaves us to do our work, she doesn't say anything, just starts talking about the equations we've been set.

'You need to get a handle on this algebra stuff,' she says. 'It's really not that hard. I'll explain it to you again.'

I sigh, frustrated. I look up and check that the teacher isn't paying attention. 'Are you all right? Last night –'

'I'm fine,' she snaps. 'Now can you please –'

'No.' I say this firmly. 'I'm sorry we nearly got caught. But we can't give up. Cari is still in danger, and we have to help her.'

'You don't have the right to tell me what I have to do!' she returns.

'We need you!' I say forcefully. 'You're incredibly smart. All that stuff you were doing with the mixers? You picked that up right away! You can help us figure this out.'

'Oh, you need my brain, is that it?' she sounds upset. 'Well, if you paid attention to anything I told you, you could work it out yourself.'

I stare at her. 'That's pretty damn mean, Sharna.'

She pulls a folded piece of paper out of her pocket. There are numbers and letters all over it, as well as a neatly-drawn graph. I stare at the letters. They're the notes of the song I played last night.

How on earth did she remember them?

'This is what you need,' she says. 'I looked up the estimated frequency of each note. It's easy enough to do that on the internet, and you can see here – this is where you broke through. I've marked the hertz value of each note –' she points to the graph – 'And I noted that when you broke through, when the thread appeared, you were playing an A minor chord. You can see the corresponding values of each note. You just need to work out how to combine them to make a stronger connection.'

She slaps the paper down in front of me and turns away.

'Sharna,' I begin, not even sure what to say, how to fix this, but she stands up abruptly, almost knocking her chair over.

'Mr Holloway?' she says. 'I'm feeling sick. I think I need to go home.'

Mr Holloway motions her over to his desk, and has a few quiet words with her. He gives her a note and she practically runs out the door.

I can't do anything but watch her leave.

***

After school, we walk to the mall. Mrs Henders isn't there yet, so we hang around outside the music store.

'I'm just wondering about those birds last night,' Keira says, leaning against one of the bare flowerbeds. 'It's almost like they were flocking on purpose, you know. Blocking the windows so we could get away.'

I shiver, because this is exactly what I was thinking.

Aaron speaks up. 'I think animals are highly tuned to the influences of the Ether.'

Keira nods. 'When I had the ice shard in my ankle, and when I used the telescope, my dog Molly went crazy.'

'So maybe the birds were drawn there by the Ether to help us?'

'Maybe not. Maybe they were just *drawn,* and it had nothing to do with helping. But it got us out of there, didn't it?'

We all agree with that.

'Have you heard from Sharna?' Keira asks me.

'No,' I shake my head. I've already told them about Sharna's disappearance, and shown them the formulas she scribbled for me. 'I don't know what's up with her! Why are girls so complicated?'

Keira punches me in the arm, and I realise it's the first time she's touched me in . . . forever. It's weird, because she's always been so hands-on. In fact, the only person I've seen her touch lately is Aaron.

'Hey,' I say to Aaron, while they others turn away, commenting on something Keira's seen in a window. 'Have you tried tracking down any of those relatives of your father yet?'

He shakes his head, looking faintly ashamed. 'I – I'm not really sure I want to, after all. I mean, they don't know me. They don't even know my dad had a son. I'm nothing to them.'

'I don't think that's true. But look, I'm happy to help. Just let me know.'

'Thank you,' he says. 'I will.'

Mrs Henders arrives, looking as batty as ever. She's wearing a long pink cardigan and a red skirt that clash horribly, and her curly grey hair is standing up. She scowls at each of us in turn, but her eyes are sparkling, and I think it's all for show. We head into the music shop.

It's a good thing we've got Mrs Henders with us. She is surprisingly conversant with the sales assistant, who quickly turns us over to Ron.

'Amplifiers,' Ron informs us, 'clarify sound quality. If you want to refine your vocal or musical output, I'd suggest Thunder Audio Speakers. We have those in our warehouse, and we can order them in for you. There are two to choose from – the TL 2000, and the TL 3000.'

'How many channels?' I break in. 'And can you select the mode?'

He looks at me like I'm a piece of chewed gum on the bottom of his shoe. He obviously likes to be the one telling the story, so I bite my tongue and let him continue.

'Most *musicians*,' he says, emphasising the word as if we, a bunch of teenagers, couldn't possibly be serious about anything let alone music, 'Choose either bridged or mono modes. Mono mode is most common, unless you're thinking of using subwoofers as well. You can also choose a stereo mode . . .'

'That's fine,' I say. 'Can we hire them?'

'What? No, of course not.' He purses his lips. 'We're a retail store.'

My heart drops. 'Well,' I say dryly. 'How much would they cost to buy?'

'I can get you a package with a pair of Premium Dual 15" PA Speakers, a pair of 18" Subwoofers, a Pair of Power Amplifiers, and the four 35' Speaker Cables for $1699. You're lucky, we're having a sale.'

Ron was probably pretty lucky none of us fainted when we heard that price. Not only because it was an insane amount of money, but because all our hopes of succeeding with this rested on us being able to get this equipment.

I can see the others look at one another. I know what they're thinking. *There's no way we can afford that.*

And before I know what I'm doing, I'm reaching into my pocket for my wallet and Mum's Visa card.

***

As we leave the shop, I realise I'm breathing hard. All the doubts I was supposed to feel as I was filling out the amount on that little scrap of paper come crashing down hard.

'I can't believe I just did that.'

'I'll be happy when we've got the stuff,' Jake says. 'Until then, we've got no guarantee this will work.'

We've arranged for the equipment to be delivered to Mrs Henders' house, because there's nowhere else they can go without people asking questions. It'll take another two days for them to be couriered out. Until then, we've just got to wait.

It's nearly dark. The others say goodbye and head for home. I'm supposed to call Anna to pick me up, but as I pull out my phone, I hesitate.

'Keira!' I call after her.

She turns back.

'Have you ever been to Sharna's house?'

'Not inside, no. She's never asked me to come over, and Mum won't let me go into that house, not since that night she called and got an earbashing from Sharna's dad.'

'But you know where she lives?'

She nods. 'Mum and I have dropped her off after school a couple of times. She lives on Nightingale Street. Number 14.'

SHARNA'S house isn't that far away. It's a pretty ordinary-looking brick house with a small front lawn. The light is on in the front room, shining through a gap in the curtains.

But there's something *not*-ordinary about the feeling of it. I start to notice some odd things. The letterbox is stuffed with mail, for one thing. There's a car in the driveway, and two of its tyres are so flat it's clear it hasn't moved in a while.

The doorbell is broken, so I knock at the door.

I listen to the sounds in the house – the thud and thump of someone moving.

The door is wrenched open and I find myself staring through the screen door at a dark and shadowy man.

He's wearing jeans and a grubby t-shirt. He's got a can of beer in one hand. He's scowling heavily, making the lines on his face deepen. I have a feeling this is his usual expression, because his eyes are hard when he looks at me.

'What do you want?' he barks, before I can say anything.

'Um – I'm here to see Sharna. I hope she's okay. I know she wasn't feeling well . . .'

He just stares at me for a moment. 'You her boyfriend?'

'No!' It bursts out. 'Um, I mean, no, sorry she's my tutor . . . Mr . . . Devon?'

He starts to laugh. It's a harsh sound, like rocks grinding together, and I wince. Maybe he's *not* her dad and I've just made an idiot out of myself.

'Hey, I like you. Come in.' He pushes open the screen door and motions me inside.

I step into a hallway that's lined with . . . well, piled *stuff*. There are plastic bags and boxes. There are computer speakers and clothes and chipped bowls and CDs and pairs of scissors, books, a packet of pencils, and just pretty much pieces of anything and everything. It all looks like it's just been put down there because no one could be bothered to put it away.

A glance into the living room shows that it's not much better, but Mr Devon leads me down the hallway. He stops at a door at the end.

'Sharna!' he bellows, pounding on the door. 'Your boyfriend's here!'

There's no response. He turns around and looks at me.

'It's probably girl trouble,' he says loudly, spilling a bit of his beer as he laughs and pats me on the shoulder. 'What's your name?'

'Mikhal,' I tell him.

'Great, great. Sharna doesn't have many friends coming around. She spends all her time flipping through books and writing and studying. You probably don't have that problem since you're being tutored, huh?'

I'm not sure what to say. 'Uh, I'm not that great at maths.'

'Good!' He laughs again, and belches loudly. 'That crap won't teach you anything about the real world. I like you, kid. You can come around any time.'

He lunges past me, heading back to the lounge room.

I'm left in a fog of sour beer and confusion. This is not how I pictured Sharna's house. I know why – she's so organised and clean. This house is the complete opposite.

The door cracks open. Sharna looks out, her face pale and her eyes narrowed. When she sees it's me, she covers her mouth with her hand and looks kind of horrified. 'Mikhal?'

'Hi,' I say awkwardly.

'You're – why did you come?'

Her eyes fill up with tears.

'Oh, wait, don't cry!' I say desperately. I don't know what to do with crying girls.

'I just – why did you have to come here? I didn't want you to . . . to see . . .'

She sniffles and steps back. I take this as an invitation to go in. And wow – it's like stepping into another house. In here I can see what's missing in the rest of the house. Sharna.

Her bed is neatly made with a plain blue quilt. There are books lined tidily on the shelves. There's a textbook open on her desk, an exercise book next to it with neat notes lining the pages. Obviously, this is what she was doing when her dad knocked on the door because she's still holding a pen in her hand.

'I was worried about you. That's all. I didn't mean to . . . intrude or anything.'

'It's not that. I don't have people over much,' she says, looking towards the lounge room, then taking the seat at the desk and leaving me the bed. 'Dad is kind of . . . I'm sorry about him.'

I smile. 'He likes me.'

She looks kind of half-relieved, half-upset. 'He didn't use to drink this much. It's gotten worse lately.'

'Sharna, I really don't care about your house or your dad or anything. I came here because I was worried about you. After last night . . .'

She suddenly folds over on herself, covering her face with her hands. She speaks in a rush. 'Mikhal, I did something stupid. I'm so . . . ashamed of myself. I should have told you. But I was scared, and mad, and . . . mostly scared . . .'

'Hey, it's okay!' I tell her. 'Whatever it is, it's okay.'

She sits there, silent, for a long minute. 'I thought we were so stupid. Especially after I saw the police show up. I hated you, and blamed you, and I kept it to myself.'

She doesn't look up.

'Do you want to tell me?' I say. 'If you don't, that's okay. But you can tell me if you want . . .'

'You're going to be mad at me.' She pulls open the drawer of her desk and pulls out a long, thin brass object. I've never seen it before but I know what it is as soon as I lay eyes on it. It's the telescope. The telescope that Mrs Henders made. That she gave to Jake, that Keira lost in the *vinarhi* when she was crossing back to our world.

Sharna sees my expression and looks like she's going to cry again. 'You are mad, aren't you?'

'No,' I say. 'But . . . how did you get this?'

'In the . . . control room, last night, when we were talking to Cari, just before I heard the noise – it was there, in the rushing waters. I didn't think it was real, didn't think it could be real until I reached out and took it.'

'Can I look at it?'

It's cold and heavy in my hands, but it feels *powerful*. The glass on the larger end is thick, and shows a reflection of the window behind me – stars are coming out in the night sky. It's beautiful.

I flip it around and look through it, through the window.

I knew I would see it.

But it still takes my breath away.

Shar. The City of Silver Light – it's real, it's there – it's in the sky, it's part of the stars, it's shining like the Moon, impossible and mysterious, elegant and graceful, incredible.

'Can you see it?' whispers Sharna.

'Yeah,' I say.

'It really is there, isn't it?'

'Yeah.'

I lower the telescope from my eyes but that doesn't erase the afterimage from my retinas.

'The reason I gave up dancing was because of Dad. When Mum left, he said it was a waste of money. That he didn't want to keep paying for something like that. And I agreed – it seemed like a waste of time. Like it wasn't important enough to justify the time and effort. So I stopped. I started looking at the environment, hoping I could find a way to fix it, all the things that are wrong, you know? And I started studying really hard, mainly maths and science.' Sharna's still looking downwards. 'Everything in maths and science makes sense. There's a reason behind it. There are formulas to follow and categories for the answers. But where does this fit into all that?'

I get it, suddenly. I understand completely why she's scared. I even know why she yelled at me. And why she didn't tell any of us about plucking the telescope out of the *vinarhi* last night. Suddenly, I get *her*. I get why she's so prickly and hard to get along with. Aaron said she was worried about things. I knew how obsessed she is with succeeding at school. It's because of this.

She's worried she's going to fail. She's not trying to please anyone else, because it's pretty clear her dad doesn't care. She wants to prove to herself that she can do it.

And this whole thing has turned all that upside down.

'That crap won't teach you anything about the real world.'

Huh. Maybe her old man's right about that one thing. Not that maths and science are crap, but that you can't expect everything in the universe to follow set rules.

'You don't have to explain anything to me,' I say. 'I'm just a freaked out by all this as you are.'

'Really?' She doesn't sound like she's convinced. 'You don't act like it. You and the others . . .'

'We've just had more time to get used to the idea, that's all. And maybe we've had it easier because we've got each other to talk to. You could have told me this before. I wouldn't have laughed at you or anything.' And the next words just fall out of my mouth. 'I really like you.'

She laughs. I would be offended, but I can tell it's a surprised laugh, a little bit hysterical. 'You *like* me?'

'Well, yeah. You're actually really a nice person. And you're . . . pretty. And smart. That's kind of hot, you know. And when you kissed me that time . . . I really liked that.'

I'm blushing, which is annoying – I never blush. But there's no stopping the red heat flooding my cheeks.

Sharna takes the telescope out of my hands and puts it on the bed. Then she leans over and kisses me again.

I think time stops.

Then her dad yells something from the lounge room. '. . . c'mon! Get the ball! . . .' and we break apart. I'm glad to see her cheeks are red, too. But it actually looks good on her.

'I told your dad I wasn't your boyfriend,' I say.

She ducks her head, embarrassed, then grins. 'Is that what we are, now? Girlfriend and boyfriend?'

I shrug. 'We could be.'

'I've never actually had a boyfriend before.'

'So maybe I can tutor you for a change,' I laugh.

'Oh, because you're such an expert?' she teases. 'I know you were going out with Toni Macquarie last year.'

I shudder. 'Yeah. I refused to use antibacterial handwash so she wouldn't hold my hand. We never even kissed because she was too afraid of my germs.'

Sharna cracks up laughing.

'I'm glad you're not afraid of my germs,' I say.

Then, suddenly, we're both looking at the telescope.

'We have to tell the others, don't we?' she says. 'They're going to hate me.'

'No,' I say with certainty. 'They're not going to hate you. But now you *have* to help us, right? We *need* you.'

She starts to say something, but I cut her off.

'Not just your brains – we need *you*. What you did last night – how you handled it when we were almost found out – that's what we need, right? Someone with guts and a clear head.' I think further on this, and add. 'Sharna, I think you're meant to be a part of this. Do you remember that day in the office, when you couldn't find those papers?'

She nods. 'Aaron told me they were in the drawer.'

'Aaron says he used the *ihlwarh* on you. It's not supposed to work on most humans, but he told me he thinks it works on people who are linked closely to the Ether. So even before any of this stuff started to happen, you were a part of it.'

She's silent for a moment, looking at her hands. 'I hope so,' she says, then looks back up at me with her eyes blazing. 'Because that means I'm worth something, right?'

I'm still holding one her hands. 'You're worth a lot more than you think. You don't need to save the whales, or the dolphins, or the planet to be worth something. You just are.'

'Wow,' she says. 'You could put that in one of your songs.'

I laugh. 'Maybe I will. I wrote a song about you, you know.'

She raises her eyebrows incredulously. 'Really? Why would you do that?'

I shrug. I don't really have an answer for that. 'I write songs about how people make me feel.'

'I'm flattered,' she says, and smiles that really pretty smile again.

***

I call Anna to pick me up, who is a bit mad that I'm late, but I tell her I had to see a friend who's sick. Mum is out doing Bridge Foundation stuff and Dad is in his study – I don't think he realises I'm not even there – so I head up to my room and call Jake.

I'm completely right. He's not angry at all.

'You *found* it?' He sounds like someone's given him all the Christmas presents he's every going to get in his life at once. 'Where is it? Have you seen the City?'

'Sharna found it. I've got it now. Yeah, I saw it. It's . . .'

'I know,' he says. 'I know what it's like. There's no word for it.'

No, I think, there's no word, but I don't tell him I reckon there might be a song to describe it. Isn't that what Mr Jackson is always saying? Songs are about things that don't have words.

'I'll call Keira,' he says, and we hang up, both of us feeling excited, exhilarated – though for different reasons.

It feels like something's swinging around inside me. I can't believe it feels this good to know Sharna likes me. I feel stupid and . . . *girly*.

I pick up the telescope and look through the window. There it is – Shar.

I clear my throat, and start to sing.

> *'I don't know why I didn't see it before*
> *All you were, all you are'*

And I can see it almost instantly, the tiny coiling thread of golden light that reaches up to the City. It's thin and it shimmers, and as soon as I stop, it's gone altogether.

I go to my desk. My little mouse friend sees me and ducks behind my lamp as I scrabble around for the page Sharna gave me yesterday. The graph of frequencies.

I open my laptop and pull up Google. She's completely right – it's not hard to find a chart of musical note frequencies for guitar. All I have to do is use the ones that resonate most strongly with Shar.

I pick up my guitar and my notebook. I open it up and start to sing.

'I don't know why I didn't see it before
All you were, all you are
It feels like I was watching you from far
away
Couldn't let myself come close...'

I pick up the telescope. And again, the golden thread glimmers, much stronger now. It takes a minute to fade instead of seconds.

I scribble it down in my notebook before I forget the tune. I tuck the notebook into my bag so I remember to take it to school in the morning and ask Sharna if she thinks I'm on the right track. Then I flop onto my bed, and somehow, I'm asleep.

Chapter Ten:
The Birds

THE birds haven't gone away. I can hear them screaming early in the morning. I pull a pillow over my head, but it doesn't work. By the time my alarm goes off I've been awake for an hour. I pull my curtains back and see them, outside the window. The sky is full of them. It's like a fluttering, screaming crowd.

I have a feeling they're watching me.

'They're directing traffic on the highway to avoid accidents,' Mum says as I head out the door with Anna. 'Just drive carefully, all right?'

Anna nods, and to prove she's listened, she drives at about thirty k's.

'Lily likes them, the birds,' she says. 'She wants to let them in the house. I have to keep locking all the doors so she won't open them.'

I laugh, but it's kind of scary, thinking of them invading houses. Would they attack anyone?

I don't know how any of us gets through the school day.

Andrew has put bubblegum all over my combination lock.

'Just so you don't lose your padlock,' he says with a grin. 'What? I'm being helpful.'

I decide to keep my bag on my back so I won't have to touch my locker. But any irritation I might have felt melts away when Sharna sits next to me in Maths. She has a very un-Sharna-like expression on her face – I recognise it from last night. Shyness.

'Hey,' she murmurs.

'I wrote a song about you,' I blurt out, then, realising that's the dorkiest thing in the world to ever admit to a girl, I groan and kick myself. 'I mean – just last night, I was thinking about you, and . . .'

I look up at her. She's smiling. It's that good smile, the one that means she's really happy. 'Can I hear it?'

'Uh, yeah. Of course. It's yours, right?'

'Did you ever write a song for Toni?'

I grin. 'Yeah! It was something like – "Glen 20 is your bestest friend, spray it and germs'll meet their end, when you hear someone sneeze, run away like a... breeze. . ."'

She snorts explosively and Mr Holloway looks up. 'Sharna! I hope Mr Wright isn't being a bad influence on you.'

She looks heartbroken for a moment. I nudge her and smile, but after that, she concentrates on her work and ignores me.

Bad influence? Pah. If only she knew.

***

We're all itching for lunch time, and when the bell rings, we practically run out the door to find Jake and Keira and Aaron. Daniel, unfortunately, is trapped across the road at his school, but Jake has been sneaky: he's made sure Daniel hid his mobile phone in his pocket, told him to hide in the bushes, and calls him once we're all together. He puts his phone on speaker so we can all talk at once.

'So, tomorrow night,' Keira says. 'It's Friday. We shouldn't have too much trouble convincing our parents to let us have a sleepover.'

'Movie night? All the Spiderman movies back-to-back or something,' I grin.

Keira rolls her eyes. 'Sharna? Will your dad let you come?'

She bites her lip and fiddles with her bag. I've got mine with me because of the bubblegum, and because I've got music after lunch, and it's easier to take my bag with me than go back down to the lockers when the bell rings for the end of the day. But I know she's brought hers with her because she's got the telescope tucked inside.

'Dad won't mind,' she says quietly. I'm pretty sure the man I met last night won't mind. 'He never minds when I'm invited out. He didn't have a problem with me going to Mikhal's party the other week. He'll probably be glad.'

I can already hear his voice.

'You mean you've actually managed to make some friends? How'd that happen?'

I clench my fists. I didn't think it was possible to hate someone you've only met once, for about ten minutes at that, but I was definitely not liking Mr Devon.

'I don't know what we'll do about the noise, though,' Keira says. 'Those speakers are going to be pretty loud.'

'We'll just have to hope the neighbours don't call the cops,' Jake says.

Daniel's voice speaks from his phone. 'Or Nina and Dad. But we can tell them we're testing equipment for the concert. Would they believe us?'

'I don't think they'd have any reason not to,' Jake agrees. His eyes are shining. 'If this works – and we get Cari back – we can really start to work things out. Especially now we've got the telescope.'

'Telescope? What –' Aaron says, bewildered.

Sharna reaches into her bag and lifts it out. It glints in the light of the cloudy day, and she holds it reverently.

That's when the birds go crazy.

***

They start to dive-bomb us from the air. I don't know if you've ever been swooped by a magpie protecting it's young, but it's not pleasant. It's only happened to me a few times. And never by fifty birds at once.

They flap and shriek as they plunge downwards. I feel the scrape of talons in my hair, the clack of a beak snapping my cheek. Someone screams – I think it's Sharna. She's grabbing her bag. Is she crazy? Forget the stupid bag! I grab her hand and drag her towards me. I can hardly see – I raise an arm over my head to shield my eyes, and lunge for the closest building. I find it more by luck than anything else, and I only realise we're there when I crash into the door with my elbow.

I shove Sharna ahead of me through the door. A wing clips my ear, and I can feel something wet on my chin. I lash out with my arm, and feel my fist connect with something solid, then I'm falling backwards into the hallway of the gym.

Sharna is underneath me.

'Sorry, sorry!' I yelp, scrambling off her. 'Are you okay?'

'Yeah,' she says, bemusedly. 'You're heavy.'

'Sorry,' I say again, looking up at the window. The bird flashes past again, once, twice, then realises it's not going to get in, and flaps away.

'What was *that*?' Sharna asks. Her face is pale. She shoves the telescope into her bag – she grabbed my bag as well, which I guess I'm grateful for. The zip is open, but I barely notice.

'You're bleeding!' I point to the long streak of blood on her arm.

'Relax. It's your blood.'

'Oh. Right.' I put a hand to my cheek and it comes away wet with sticky red stuff. It can't be too bad, though, because it doesn't hurt a bit.

Maybe that's just the shock.

'Mikhal?'

It's Mr Jackson. He looks very concerned.

'What happened?'

'It was the birds. And yes, I know that sounds crazy.'

His lips press into a thin line, and I can tell he doesn't think it sounds insane. 'I saw it from the window. I meant to ask what you were doing when they attacked you. Anything unusual?'

'What could we be doing that makes birds attack us?' Sharna says, but even as the words leave her mouth I realise how weird it is that he would ask that. As if he knows somehow, or at least suspects what we were doing. Sharna goes on. 'We were just eating lunch . . . maybe they were hungry or something.'

Mr Jackson rubs a hand over his chin, like he's trying to decide whether we're telling the truth.

'Mr Jackson? Mikhal probably needs to go to the nurse.'

'Oh, right, of course.' He shakes himself, as if this hadn't even occurred to him. 'Okay, go on. I'll go and check the grounds.'

But he doesn't go through the doors. He's still standing there, peering outside thoughtfully as we head down the corridor to the nurse's room.

***

Not long after we step into the nurse's room, there's an announcement over the PA system that all students are to stay inside for the rest of lunch. The corridors become crowded, and everyone's talking about how we were attacked.

Once we're around the corner, I text Jake and he tells me that he, Keira and Aaron are fine – they're in the library, but Jake's worried because his phone, the old one we're using to contact Cari, is now scratched and dented by beaks and claws. *Just hope it still works. Weird – they went nuts when Sharna pulled out the telescope.*

That *is* weird. It's like the birds knew exactly what it was, and they didn't like it. Or didn't want us to use it.

***

The school has a hard time getting all the students home that night. Teachers are on guard duty with hockey sticks and cricket bats. It would be funny if it wasn't for the memory of those black wings flapping at my face, and the lingering sting of betadine on my cheek.

We're mentioned that night on the news, as 'several students who were attacked during the afternoon'. They're saying that there's a chance they may need to use 'extreme methods' to cull the bird population. But since no one else has been attacked, the environmental protection people are up in arms.

Some locals have started taking matters into their own hands. Ron, the manager of the music store, is arrested for trying to get the birds to move from his store front by setting off firecrackers – his excuse was that the bird droppings were a health and safety hazard

'If this goes on, we might have to rethink having this concert outside,' Mum says, and I feel a sudden clenching in my chest.

'Oh, that reminds me,' I say as I pull Mum's Visa card out of my wallet. 'I used the card.'

The half-lie is twisting inside me. It's not a full lie, because I don't say what I used it out for, but it feels horrible.

Mum nods. 'Oh, how much?'

'Um, one thousand seven hundred.'

'Great! Great.' She's distracted, I can tell. I take advantage of that and retreat to my room.

I'm looking through my bag for my notebook, and I realise it's not there.

I must have dropped it when the birds attacked.

Chapter Eleven:
Search and Rescue

I GET Anna to drop me off at school early. 'Can I go straight to Jake's after school?' I ask her. 'I've got my stuff packed.'

'Your mum told me about your sleepover,' she said.

'It's not a sleepover!' I tell her. 'It's a movie night. We're too old for sleepovers.'

Anna laughs.

I step out into the grounds warily. But even though the birds watch me, they don't make a move, so my confidence grows.

But even though I search the whole area around where we were sitting yesterday lunchtime, I can't find my notebook. I don't know what could have happened to it.

I guess that's what you get for carrying it around everywhere, I think to myself. Now Andrew will probably find it. That's all you need.

For last period, we have Science, and Sharna sits at the back with me, and I'm almost glad we're doing theory, because it means I get to sit next to her the whole time. I watch Jake, Keira and Aaron who are sitting in front of us. Keira and Aaron have their heads bent together and they're laughing about something. Jake is politely looking away. The rest of the class is distracted.

'So, if you add more oxygen . . .' Sharna is saying when I prop my folder up on my desk and lean over to kiss her on the cheek.

She's startled, then bats me away. 'What are you doing?'

'Being distracted.' I say.

And that's when Andrew walks past my desk and dumps a bottle of indicator dye on my text book.

I'm on my feet in an instant. 'What the hell?' I yell. I can't help it. It's all way too much. I've put up with this all week. I can't keep ignoring it – he's just going to keep doing it. And besides, I'm mad. I'm really mad.

'Oh, I'm sorry,' says Andrew. 'Did I interrupt your little make out session?' He turns to Sharna. 'Why are you with him?'

'Are you jealous because you want him?' Sharna snaps back, trying to mop up the dye with some tissues from her bag. It's the same one, I realise, that she's been keeping the telescope in, and she must still have it in there, because she refuses to put it in her locker. 'Seriously. Just give up, Andrew.'

Andrew doesn't like that. 'I was going to say you could do better,' he says. 'But I guess if you can see something in a loser like him, you're probably the perfect couple. Or is it just his money you're after?'

That strikes a chord with Sharna. She picks up my textbook and heaves it at Andrew's head.

It hits with a solid thwack. It's a heavy textbook.

***

We both get sent down the Beige Mile to Mrs Hildebrand's office.

'You know,' she says. 'I really thought putting your two together was a good idea. But I see I might have been mistaken. Sharna, I've got a good mind to call your dad –'

'No!' she yells.

Both of us are startled. Mrs Hildebrand's glasses slip down her nose, and she pushes them back up, absently.

'It's just . . . he's probably sleeping,' she amends. 'Please, please, just don't . . . don't wake him up.'

I can hear the fear in Sharna's voice, and my heart is in my throat. There is something more than she's telling me.

'It's my fault,' I say quickly.

'I've had reports from your teachers,' she says. 'You two are talking in class and distracting one another. This is not why I put you together.'

'But my grades have gone up!' I protest. 'I got a B on that maths test. And I'm working really hard. I'm organising this big concert –'

'Your extracurricular activities were meant to improve your work, not create further distractions.' She purses her lips. Then her voice lowers into a calm murmur. 'I've heard about the concert. It's a great idea, Mikhal, and I'm glad you're doing this and enjoying it. But I can't overlook this. You'll have detention after school for the next week, okay? I'll call your mother.'

No, I scream inwardly. But I grit my teeth and don't protest. She can't call Sharna's dad. If the idea of it makes her look like that – she can't call Sharna's dad.

The final bell rings.

'I have a meeting right now,' she says. 'But I'll be calling your mother first thing on Monday. I want you to take this detention form home with you now,' she says, pulling out a dreaded pink slip and scribbling something on it.

All I can do is thank whatever forces there are out there that Mum's not going to find out tonight, or I'd never be able to go to our sleepover. Or movie night. Or whatever we decide to call it.

***

I look sideways at Sharna as we leave the office, but her eyes are downcast.

'You didn't have to do that,' she says.

'Well, I couldn't let her call your dad. Obviously.' I wish I could use the *ihlwarh* on her. I wish I could know what she's thinking.

'He doesn't hit me or anything, if that's what you're thinking.' She says this in her usual strong voice, but I can tell that inside she's still reeling from her near miss. 'He wouldn't do that. He wouldn't even care about me getting in trouble. He'd laugh and say *'at last you're acting like a normal teenager'*. But if she called him and woke him up – he'd probably go off. He'd yell at her. He'd tell her to mind her own business and call her an old bag. At the very least.'

I grimace. 'Well, it'd be true.'

She grins, and I'm relieved to see the spark in her eyes.

***

We all arrive at Mrs Henders place at almost exactly the same time. Sharna has walked, Keira went straight there with Aaron – she's been spending more time with him than she has at her own house, so it's not unusual for her – and Jake had picked Daniel up at his school, stopped by to pick up their stuff, and is coming up the driveway just as Anna is dropping me and my guitar off.

Daniel points to the sky. 'The birds are back.'

He's right. There are birds gathering in the bushes on the nature strip, and in the trees in the park, almost making the trees sway under their weight. Mrs Henders pink flamingo garden ornaments are looking a little shabby, covered in droppings.

'Are they following us?' I ask no one in particular. 'I swear they're following us.'

'Aaron says they delivered the stuff this afternoon,' Jake says. 'The delivery guy wanted to stay around and set it up – in Mrs Henders lounge room.'

I laugh.

I'm itching to see it. Apart from the equipment in the studio at school, I've never had access to a complete, professional speaker system before. And when we walk into the house, I'm overwhelmed by the sight of those beautiful speakers, the gleaming amplifiers, and neatly coiled cords.

Mrs Henders doesn't look thrilled.

'I don't know why all this has to be so *big*,' she says, coming down the hallway and edging past one of the subwoofer speakers that won't fit in the lounge room. 'Sometimes I miss Shar, if only because humans are so uneconomical with space.'

She scowls and mutters. But she makes us dinner of spaghetti with homemade sauce, and even lets us eat it in the lounge room in front of the TV. I think we've worn down her standoffishness, at last.

We're all eager to get started, of course, but she won't let us do anything until we've all finished what's on our plates. Even though it's delicious, I don't have much of an appetite. I just keep glancing over at those speakers.

It's completely dark outside by the time were ready to start moving the stuff to the pagoda. This is good, because it means everyone's off the street, in their homes, with their curtains pulled shut against the winter night.

The park is dark and deserted.

Except for the birds.

More and more of them are gathering in the trees. I try to ignore them, concentrating on the frigid night air burning in my lungs, the dew from the grass soaking into the cuffs of my jeans. The pagoda looms out of the shadows, the lights from the street picking out the delicate ironwork and glinting off the plastic sheeting covering the open sides.

'Do you know how to set all this stuff up?' asks Keira, huffing as she hauls one of the amplifiers up the steps and sets it on the concrete.

'I've got a basic idea, but ... not really,' I admit. I'm not one for reading instructions, but Sharna, of course, has the diagrams laid out on the seat that rings the edge of the pagoda before we start and is busy directing everyone. Soon the neatly coiled leads are uncoiled and not so neat, but at least they're in the right plugs, and I'm getting a pleasing sound when I tap the microphone.

It's a strange sound. The frosty air gives it more clarity. 'It sounds *good*,' I say. It really does. I give it a few tests and I nearly curl up and die, I'm so impressed.

I want to turn the volume dial right up – into the red danger blow-your-eardrums-out area – but I restrain myself. We don't need to call too much attention to what we're doing. Instead I arrange all the speakers so they're in a u-shape, facing the archway of the pagoda, where Jake is setting up the phone in the middle of the floor.

Sharna pulls the telescope out of her bag.

Outside, the birds start to shriek.

'They don't like the telescope,' Aaron says. He's eyeing the thing in Sharna's hands. 'Can I use it? Just for a moment?'

I can see the hope and longing in his eyes. He wants to look at the City, I realise. He wants to look at his home and make sure it's still there.

Mrs Henders, rubbing her hands together to warm them, edges her way up the steps. She draws in a breath at the sight of the telescope.

'It is yours, isn't it?' Sharna says, shyly. 'It's beautifully made.'

'That thing,' Mrs Henders growls, sitting on the wooden bench seat next to one of our discarded cardboard boxes. 'I would give any-thing not to have made it. I only hope it can be used for good, now.'

'If this works –' Jake begins, but he's cut off as something thumps into the plastic sheeting to our right. Hard.

At first I think someone's thrown a rock, but then there's another loud noise, and I see the bird dropping away and coming back for another round. The plastic is dented, but it's durable stuff, and hasn't torn.

'Oh, no!' Sharna gasps.

'We can't stop,' Jake reminds us grimly. 'Cari is counting on us!'

'Mikhal, are you ready?' Keira asks.

'No,' I answer honestly, but I know it's time. I pluck a few notes. I strum a chord. I listen to the amazingly clear sound that echoes off into the night, then lean forward into the microphone and start to sing.

'I'm coming around
To your point of view
Might take me a while to get through'

It's a kind of stupid song to choose – one of my less miserable ones, with a cheerful melody that I worked out one day when I was mucking around in my room. I don't know why it comes out when I start to play, but for some reason it does, and as I continue, I realise why I picked it.

The mood of the song is hopeful.

We all feel it. Jake and Daniel are staring at the phone. Keira, her crystal shard clutched tightly in one hand, is holding Aaron's hand with the other. Sharna is biting her lip and holding the telescope tightly, looking at me. Mrs Henders old eyes are crinkling up at the edges as she clutches the fabric of her skirt.

We're pouring all our hope into this little space.

And it starts to work.

The rushing sound of the *vinarhi* spreads out around us. It fills the pagoda with moving silver light. It feels soft, like silk against our skin.

I switch songs. I start the one I wrote last night – the one that I wrote for Sharna, using the music that resonates with the City. I breathe it in, the *vinarhi*, weave it with my song.

I can see Keira doing the same opposite me. She's concentrating so hard there's sweat on her forehead. I hear another thud and another and I know more birds are hitting the plastic – not just the walls, but the poles as well, and scratching at the roof, cawing like there's no tomorrow – but I don't let myself stop. I just keep playing.

> *'If you let me, maybe I'll see*
> *Another way ahead'*

'I can see it!' Aaron says. The telescope glints in the dim light as he traces the sky with it. 'I can see the thread! It reaches all the way from the City . . .'

A voice answers hers, a girl's voice, thin and reedy. 'Thread? I can see . . .'

'Cari?' Jake says.

'. . .I'm still here . . .' It's Cari's voice, and it's clearer than it's ever been before. 'But . . . I think I'm forgetting . . .'

'Cari, we're trying to build a bridge for you.' Keira calls. 'Can you see us? Can you make your way towards us?'

'. . . I don't know where I am . . . the shield around me is failing . . . I want to go home . . .'

She sounds scared and lost and alone and afraid, and very, very young. I can't stop playing.

Jake speaks loudly and calmly, though I know inside he's shaking. 'Cari, you're going to have to step through the shield.'

'. . . but it's bad out there! I don't want this . . . oh . . . who are you? How can you speak to me?'

'Cari, it's me,' Jake says desperately. The rushing, foaming stuff that is the *vinarhi* swirls around us, and I can see things through it, now, dark shapes and silhouettes that are not the trees of the park or the cars in the distance. Are they people? Animals? They might be either, or both.

My vision blurs, as if I'm looking through several panes of glass, and then everything shifts dizzyingly. I know I'm seeing other worlds, then. I'm seeing all the other countless dimensions that exist. They're all connected here at this moment.

Keep playing . . .

Keira is working hard. The crystal shard glimmers and glistens as she waves it this way and that. She's catching my notes with it and weaving them together.

And then I see it, the golden thread. It's as thick as a rope now. It's strong enough to be seen, even without the telescope, though Aaron still clenches the precious thing tightly in his fist, looking upwards. As I play, more and more strands wrap themselves around it, binding tighter, making it thicker, stronger.

It goes all the way up through the archway of the pagoda, up into the night sky, but all I can see is the rushing white light.

And then I see her.

Rebecca.

Cari.

She looks just like she did that night we went out to the mall all those weeks ago, when I didn't know who she was at all – but she's thinner, and so pale she's almost transparent, like she's a ghost or something. She's wearing a thin white shift and crouching just inside the edge of a curving, bluish field of flickering energy.

I know what that energy is. I remember it from what Keira and Aaron showed me. On Shar, everyone can see it – the colours of a person's mood and identity. Her own lifeforce. It's all that's keeping her from being swept away to those who-knows-where worlds.

And it's failing.

'Cari, you have to listen to me. Can you hear me? Answer me if you can,' Jake says. 'Just say something.'

'Jake?' She sounds very tired.

'Oh, thank God, Cari,' Jake says. 'I thought I'd lost you.'

'I'm here,' she says. 'I'm here.'

It's hard to see, but Keira is plucking at my notes faster now. She's winding them around each other. The thread curves under its own weight, but it's not a thread anymore, it's a path. It's a bridge.

Jake speaks. 'Cari, you're going to have to let go. You're going to have to lower the shield around you so you can step onto the bridge.'

'Can't let go . . . it's too fast . . . it will take me!'

'No. Just step through onto the bridge.'

'Cari?' Daniel calls. 'I don't like swimming, either. But when I went to the swimming pool, Nina told me to just take a deep breath and plunge in and not think about it. And it kind of worked. I was still scared, but I did it.'

'Dan . . . Daniel?' she says.

'Remember in Neon Genesis Evangelion, Cari?' Daniel goes on. 'Remember how you watched it with me? Shinji didn't really want to be an Evangelion pilot. He was crazy scared! But he did it. It was hard to believe he could do it, but he did.'

If only she can step onto the bridge. She'll be okay if she can do that.

Keep playing.

Cari stands up. She wavers a little. She's still so far away, and she almost seems to fade a little bit more, to become less solid. Then she steps onto the golden bridge. Her blue aura-shield flickers and dissipates.

Daniel keeps talking. 'I've got all the second season. You can watch them with me. We'll have a marathon. And there's this new Xbox game – you can play it with me and Aaron, because Jake totally sucks.'

Cari is laughing. She takes another unsteady step. The bridge sways and bucks under her bare feet, but she keeps going, following Daniel's voice.

The closer she gets, the more solid she seems to become, until, finally, she's only a few steps away. We're all watching her, all urging her onwards wordlessly. And then Aaron pulls away from Keira. He takes a step towards the Bridge, and Cari.

'I can see it!' he says. 'I can see the City. I can see Shar!'

'Aaron, come back!' Keira yelps. 'Don't step on it – I don't think the bridge will hold both of you – it's not strong enough.'

Cari reaches the end of the bridge and steps down out of the mist onto the grass to one side of the steps. She sways back and forth and then slumps to her knees. The grass crackles around her, bursting into little flickers of flame that die just as quickly.

Everything is chaos, then. Jake is at her side, instantly, shouting – is she okay, is she hurt, can she open her eyes? – and Sharna is with him, pulling Cari's long blond hair back over her shoulder. Daniel is pumping the air with his fist in victory, and I'm shoving the guitar aside.

Aaron is standing up, looking at the place where the broken threads of the bridge are unravelling, becoming nothing, falling away. 'I could have gone,' he says forlornly. 'I should have gone back.'

I'm not listening to him, because I can see something in the street. A set of car headlights flicking off. Who is it? Did they see what was happening? They couldn't have been there long, surely. They couldn't have seen anything.

The *vinarhi* is already dissolving. Even as the noise vanishes, I'm aware of how quiet it is. Something's changed.

The birds aren't singing, cawing, or fluttering their wings. It's completely silent.

Chapter Twelve:
The Battle Begins

I WALK slowly down the steps and crouch next to Jake. We both look down at Cari.

'We have to get her inside,' he says. He reaches for her, heedless of the steaming embers around her. 'She must be –'

'She's from Shar,' Keira says. 'She doesn't feel the cold the way we do, remember?'

It's true. Though she's unconscious, she's not shivering.

Jake reaches under her, gently lifting her from the ground. As he does, I notice something on the grass. Everyone is following Jake, anxiously watching Cari. Sharna turns around and looks for me.

'What is that?'

She comes beside me to stare at what I've seen. We both peer closely at the centre of the burned patch of grass.

It's a tiny little silver flower.

Even as the last wisps of the *vinarhi* fades, it vanishes from sight.

***

Later that night, we're sprawled out in our sleeping bags, exhausted but elated. I catch snippets of whispered conversations as I drift in and out of sleep.

Keira's voice is soft. 'Would you really have gone?'

Aaron's answering murmur is barely audible. 'I wanted to. I wish I didn't, but I miss my home, Keira.'

There is silence for a while.

'I would miss you,' Keira says.

If I twist to look over my shoulder I can see Cari, who is lying on the couch, deep in sleep. Jake is sitting propped up next to her. It's clear he's not going to be sleeping tonight. He doesn't want to take his eyes off her.

Daniel keeps turning over and over, huffing and sighing, trying to find sleep.

And Sharna . . .

In the silver moonlight coming through the window, Sharna looks perfect.

As if she realises I'm looking at her, she blinks her eyes open sleepily. 'We did do it, didn't we? I'm not just dreaming all this?'

I don't answer her, because I'm not really sure it's not a dream.

'We saved her,' she answers herself instead. 'I'm glad we did it.'

I am, too.

***

The next morning is when the craziness really starts.

Mrs Henders wakes us, clattering around in the kitchen with preparations for breakfast. Sunlight streams in through the frost-rimmed window. The birds are there – I see them when I sit up and rub the grit out of my eyes – but they're silent. They flutter their wings lazily, as if they're not quite sure what to do with the day.

'Is she awake?' Keira asks.

I turn to the couch. Cari is still lying there. In the light of day she looks much more like a real person. Jake has fallen asleep holding her hand, and as she stirs now, he lets her go and looks slightly embarrassed.

'Jake?' she says.

His face lights up. 'I'm so glad you're here. I'm so glad you're okay.'

'I feel . . . strange.' She looks at the window, and I see tears flood her eyes. I know she's looking for the City, but here, in the daylight, without the telescope, it can't be seen. 'Am I really here?'

'Yes.'

'I'm sorry I had to leave you.'

'You had to do what was right.'

'But I didn't succeed. They're coming, Jake. They're going to destroy everything.'

'The battle's not over yet,' Jake says and we all have to laugh at that clichéd movie-line.

***

Morning comes late. The birds don't sing as the sun finally comes over the horizon. The world seems strangely quiet for a Saturday, and when I look out the window I see that the sky is clear, but the birds are still fluttering around aimlessly.

I edge my way past the speakers, which we piled hastily into the lounge room after our efforts last night. The others are in the kitchen, helping Mrs Henders make enough toast for all of us, so I'm alone when I pick up the telescope and look through the window.

I'm treated to a view of the Phoenix Park. I tilt the telescope up to the sky. There it is – the City of Silver Light. The bridge is gone, and so are any signs that anything happened last night at all. It's strange that no one else noticed anything. I suddenly think of the car headlights I'd seen going past, but I'm pretty sure they would have been too far away to see anything.

I can see the pagoda, looking very inconspicuous after last night's drama. And then . . .

'Hey!' I call out. Daniel drifts in first, munching on a slice of toast.

'Look through this,' I say, shoving it at him.

'Look near the pagoda.'

He squints into the telescope and sees what I'm looking at instantly. His eyes go wide. 'Geez! What is that?'

At the sound of his voice, the others come in, and as the telescope is passed around, everyone does a double-take when they see what's happening in the park.

It's a white tree.

The tiny little flower I'd seen last night has shot up in just a few hours. It's already as tall as the real trees around it. I can almost see it growing as I watch.

'It's just like the trees in Shar,' Keira murmurs. 'They grow them from seed-crystals.'

'How can that be?' Aaron says. 'Those trees have never grown here before.'

'But that's the spot where the Bridge ended. Where Cari came through.' Keira says. 'Could that have caused it?'

'A Sharian tree can't grow without a crystal.' Cari says this with certainty.

'It's beautiful,' Sharna says.

That's when my phone rings, interrupting us. I look back through the window, but the tree can't be seen without the telescope. I turn my attention to the incoming call.

It's Mum. She doesn't sound happy.

'I'm sending Anna to pick you up, Mikhal.'

'Mum, I'm not ready to come home yet –'

'She'll be there in ten minutes,' she says firmly. There's no arguing with her.

***

I tell Aaron that we'll stop back to pick him up later, to take him out to Swan Lakes. I don't want to bring him with me, since I'm not going to use anyone as a buffer for Mum's anger again.

I know it's bad news even when I walk into the house.

Mum's waiting for me in the lounge room, sitting on the edge of the couch with her hands in her lap.

That's not good.

Down the hallway, I can see Dad. He's talking to someone who I can't quite see because whoever it is, they're standing in the doorway to the kitchen.

His voice sounds distant and serious.

That's not good, either.

'Mikhal,' Mum says, beckoning me into the lounge room. A mouse scuttles over her shoe, and she kicks it away with a noise of disgust. 'I've spent all week arranging catering for the concert next Saturday. I've organised a magician's act and a drinks stall and some sideshow games. I just called Mr Miles to ask about arrangements for the band.'

Uh oh.

My heart sinks all the way down into the floor. Further. Into the earth under the house.

'He said he hadn't made the arrangements because he was never asked to.'

Further. It's almost gone entirely. I'm left with a ringing in my ears that is something like I felt after Andrew tried to blast my eardrums out.

'He said you never gave him my card details, Mikhal. But I told you I checked with the bank. The card was charged one thousand seven hundred dollars.'

I wonder if I can sit down but I can't remember how my legs work.

'What did you do with the money, Mikhal?'

'I – uh –'

I don't know what I would have said, but it turns out I don't get the chance. Dad enters, trailing a man behind him.

I gape in surprise. It's Mr Jackson.

'Hello, Mikhal.' He smiles, but there's something strained about it. I stare at him in horror. Teachers are not ever supposed to enter your home. It's an unwritten rule.

'Um,' I say, my eyes darting from Mum to Dad to Mr Jackson and wondering what's going on.

'I've asked your parents if I can have a word with you about your movements,' Mr Jackson says. 'I'm a little bit concerned about you, Mikhal.'

'Why?'

'Well, as you know,' Mr Jackson's gaze is piercing and he stares at me openly. Though his tone is light I can tell he's desperate to hear my answer. 'I take a particular interest in the wellbeing of my students. Now, yesterday evening, I was passing the park – the Phoenix Park, just over the bridge. And I believe I saw you and your friends gathering in the pagoda.'

My absent heart gives a frantic spurt of movement, but I can hardly feel it. The head-lights. Of course it was him. But . . . why was he at the park? Was he just driving past, like he says? Or was he spying on us? That's crazy, I think. I'm being paranoid. He couldn't possibly know what we're doing, or why.

This thought gives me strength. Suddenly I feel incredibly calm. I know what I have to say.

I look Mum in the eyes. She's more worried than angry, I see.

'We were preparing for the concert.'

Confusion. Mum's eyebrows furrow. 'What?'

'The concert. Mum, I used the cheque you gave me to buy some speaker systems and equipment.'

'But . . .' she flounders. 'But I gave you the card to book the band. Why did you buy equipment? Who's going to use it?'

'Well,' I say, and this is the hard part, 'I am.'

There. I've said it. No taking it back now.

I look at Dad. He looks as stunned as Mum does. Mr Jackson cocks his head to one side. He looks relieved, almost, and actually happy. This puts doubt back in my mind. If he didn't know anything about what we're doing, he wouldn't actually care so much that our actions were supposedly so innocent. 'That's wonderful,

Mikhal. I'm so glad to see you've decided to take your music seriously.'

I shrug. My face is burning, and I'm wondering what on earth I've gotten myself into.

Chapter Thirteen:
A Tree Grows in the Park

I CALL Sharna on the way back to Mrs Henders's place. She doesn't answer. I call again, but her phone is turned off. I'm itching with this news.

'I don't see why you didn't tell me,' Mum says as she drives. 'I wish you'd told me what you were doing with the money, and checked with me first. But the way it's worked out, well...'

'I didn't think you'd go for it,' I reply. 'I thought it was probably best if I just did it, then I couldn't back out.'

'Hm,' Mum says. 'Well, at least you've got Mr Jackson on your side. He seems like a nice teacher. Very concerned about you, and your music.'

I try calling Sharna again, even though we're already pulling into Mrs Henders's street. Still no answer.

'Just be a minute,' I tell Mum as I get out of the car.

But Sharna's not there. When I'm back in

the lounge room, Keira tells me the others have all gone home. It's only Keira and Aaron waiting for me.

'Really?!' Keira shoots up from the couch and claps her hands. 'That's brilliant! That way we've already covered the costs of the concert.'

'Yeah, except that I don't know if I can do this.'

'Don't start doubting yourself – you can do it. I know you can. I'll get started on the posters. We can do it next weekend. We're pretty much set to go now we've got all the equipment.'

My mouth is dry and I frantically change the subject. 'How's Cari?'

'She's fine. She went home with Jake. She's going to stay here with Mrs Henders and Aaron for now.'

'I've been trying to call Sharna. Did she go home?'

'Yeah, soon after you left. She was packing up her bag, and the next thing I knew she'd jumped up and said she had to go. She wouldn't let anyone drive her. She practically ran out the door. I don't get her, sometimes.'

I don't think anyone will ever get Sharna.

'I'm a bit worried about her, Mikhal,' she goes on in a softer voice. 'I was holding the crystal shard and I could see her aura when she was going through her bag. It flashed red, like she was angry. She was pretty upset when she left.'

'I'll try calling her again.'

But again, she doesn't answer, and Mum honks the horn from outside. 'We better go,' I tell Aaron.

Keira squeezes Aaron's arm as he stands up. 'Are you sure you don't want me to come?' she asks.

He shakes his head. 'I'm not sure what these people will say. They might not be his relatives at all.'

***

The drive isn't long – just over half an hour. Aaron spends most of his time looking through the window. I can't tell if he's interested in the scenery – I guess this is probably the most he's seen of our world so far – or if he's just trying not to think about anything else.

Finally, we pull up in front of a low brick house. It's old, and it looks a bit shabby – the tin roof is buckled and peeling, and the fence has been propped up with what looks like an old broom handle. But there are signs that it's been cared-for, too. A few neat flowerbeds, even though the flowers are all blackened, dead because of the frost. There's a wind chime hanging beside the door, and the letterbox has been painted with the name 'Lovell'.

Mum turns off the engine and we sit.

'Are you ready to go in?' she asks, but Aaron doesn't move for a moment.

'I –'

Suddenly there's movement. The door opens, and a young girl comes out. She's dressed in a parka, bright red, and her hands are in oversized mittens.

'Don't go too far,' someone calls, and a moment later a woman joins her, closing the door behind her. It must be the girl's mum. She's tall, and she has dark hair. Except for that, she looks a lot like Aaron.

'Wow,' I say. 'That could be your aunty.'

Aaron's eyes are on the little girl. She's running ahead, laughing in that way kids have, when they're just having fun. I wonder what Aaron's thinking. Maybe that this could have been him. From what he said about life in Shar, from what he showed me, there's not a lot of time for little kids to run around and just be kids.

'Aaron?' Mum says.

'I think we should just go,' he says, suddenly.

'Are you sure?' Mum sounds disappointed, and I admit, I am, too.

'Yes,' Aaron says. 'I'm sure. Please, can we just go?'

Mum starts the car again, and we pull away. Aaron keeps his eyes straight ahead.

***

In my room, I find my mouse friend waiting

for me on my desk. It's been nibbling at one of my textbooks.

I try calling Sharna again. No answer.

So I take another deep breath. 'Okay,' I tell my mouse friend. 'I can do this.'

I dial Andrew's number.

'What the hell do you want?' he fires at me as soon as he picks up.

'I've got a proposition for you.' I try to keep my voice even, though I want to answer him in the same rude tone. 'I'm organising a concert for the charity drive.'

'Oh, yeah, I've heard about your little sing-along. Sounds great . . . not. What's it got to do with me?'

'I'm playing.' I blurt it out. 'And I need back-up. On drums.'

There's a long silence. 'Are you joking?'

'No. You're good on the drums.' It takes effort to say this, because I know I'm stoking his ego, but it's true. 'I know you hate me, but there's no reason we can't work on some of the songs I've written, right? We hardly even have to talk. Besides. Mrs Hildebrand loves this stuff. It might get you out of detention.'

That gets him. 'Oh yeah?' He sounds thoughtful. 'Okay. You said you've got some songs?'

***

Saturday night passes, and Sunday comes. I spend a lot of time in my room with my mouse – and three of his buddies – dialling Sharna's number and waiting for her to answer. She doesn't.

To fill the time in between, I sit down and play some of my songs. I've got a lot of work to do if I'm going to get them ready by next weekend. It's hard without my notebook. I can't remember bits and pieces. I kick myself again for losing it.

In the end I pick five of my best, and three of my not-so-best songs. I'll just have to rewrite some of them – I'm missing the chorus on one of them, and for the life of me I can't remember the opening chords on *Silver Lining*. Not to mention, I'll have to work out the drums with Andrew.

But with seven songs, the magician's act, and all the other stuff, I figure we'll have earned the $10 we're charging per ticket.

Maybe.

What if everyone thinks I'm crap? *I* think I'm crap! Everyone else will just think I'm *twice* as crap.

I look at Roger on his stand. He's taunting me.

My phone goes off. I pick it up, expecting Jake, or maybe Andrew, so I don't glance at the caller ID.

'Hello?'

'How could you do that?' Sharna's voice explodes in my ear. 'How could you?'

'Hey – what?'

'Oh, yeah, pretend you don't know!' She's crying. Her voice is high-pitched, almost hysterical. 'You know exactly what you think of me. The only problem is that now I do too.'

She's sobbing into the phone.

'I just don't know how you could write that and then tell me you liked me. I believed you, Mikhal.'

These words are whispered, and then the phone goes dead.

I stare down at it, wondering what on earth just happened. What did I write?

The mouse and his friends chitter in answer. I think they're laughing at me.

***

I don't know how long I've been lying there when my phone rings again. I grab it, thinking it might be Sharna, but Keira's voice echoes in my ear urgently.

'It's growing.'

'Keira,' I say, annoyed. 'You're going to have to learn how to explain yourself properly.'

'The tree, Miky! The freaking Sharian tree. It's . . . really growing. Can you come to Jake's place?'

I don't bother to ask for permission from Mum. I grab my bike and ride.

***

Keira, Cari and Aaron are waiting for me at Mrs Henders. Keira wrenches open the door. 'Jake and Daniel are out with Nina, but I've texted them,' she says, grabbing my elbow and dragging me into the lounge room. 'Sharna, too.'

'Did she – did she reply?' I ask her, trying not to sound desperate.

Keira shakes her head. She grabs something off the coffee table. 'I found this on the floor. It's yours, isn't it? It must have fallen out of your bag this morning.'

I snatch it. 'My notebook! Thank God. I thought I'd lost it when the –'

When the birds attacked. Suddenly, everything clicks into place. It all comes to me in a rush. Sharna must have picked it up when we were running for cover, shoved it in her bag by mistake. When she was going through her bag this morning at Mrs Henders place she must have found it. And read it.

I told her I wrote a song about how she made me feel.

She must have read the one I wrote when I was mad at her.

But . . . I wrote those good songs about her, too. Didn't she read them? Did she only read that one? Suddenly the words pop into my head, clear as day, without me having to try and remember.

'You're reaching for something impossible
A dream is just a dream because you'll
always wake
Can't you see how much you frustrate me?
Making me feel like I can only fail
But you're the one who'll disappoint me'

'Ugh!' I groan to myself, hitting my forehead with the palm of my hand. 'How did this happen?'

'What?' Keira asks.

'Nothing,' I mumble. 'Just tell me what's happening.'

We sit in Mrs Henders' lounge room, aiming the telescope through the window. It's amazing.

The tree hasn't just grown. It's exploded. It's shot up above the roof of the pagoda. Its branches are spreading out like winding tentacles. It doesn't even look like a tree now.

'It's kind of pretty,' Keira says, but her voice is worried.

Mrs Henders looks grave. She takes a turn with the telescope, pointing it at the tree, then leans back shaking her head.

'This shouldn't be happening,' Aaron says.

I take the telescope again. A branch unfolds, reaching upwards like one of those motion-capture movies that show flowers growing at incredible rates.

Except this isn't a nature documentary. It's real.

'Daniel and I saw trees like this in Shar,' Keira says. 'They grew just as quickly. But I don't know how one got here. I didn't even know they could grow in our world.'

'Neither did I,' Cari replies, and even Mrs Henders looks stumped.

***

First thing on Monday, I duck down the Beige Mile into the office. Mrs Hildebrand is just coming in, juggling her car keys and handbag and a stack of folders.

'Mrs Hildebrand!' I call. 'I just want to talk to you about –'

She holds up a hand. 'I don't want to hear it, Mikhal. I'm still going to have to call your parents.'

'No, no! Go ahead, I mean. Call them if you need to. But I just need to ask you something about my extracurricular stuff, you know the concert that's going to be held this Saturday? I'm wondering if I can put flyers up around the school. And, also, with the detention – I'm just wondering about how long we're going to be in there for. Andrew and I are going to be playing, so we need to practise –'

Her eyes brighten. 'Oh, that's a great idea!' She looks at me shrewdly. 'I have a feeling you're doing this to get out of your punishment, Mikhal.'

I start to tell her that I'm totally not, but she cuts me off again.

'But I want to support you in this, as well. Especially if it means you're working cooperatively with Andrew. I'm willing to allow you to use the time you would have spent in detention to practise and to produce flyers or anything else you need to do. I'll talk to Mr Jackson about you using the music room after school. If you can do this without getting into trouble, it will count significantly towards your extra credit.'

I have to stop myself from pumping my fist in the air.

***

I wait all day for Sharna to show up.

She doesn't come.

I don't think she's ever missed a full day of school, and I'm worried.

***

Andrew is happy to hear that we're no longer on detention. We meet for our first practice session after school.

Mr Jackson is waiting for us in the end music room. 'I thought you boys might like to use the studio,' he says.

We agree. Both of us are a bit nervous, I think; I much prefer this doubtful Andrew to the angry one I punched in the jaw the other week, so I'll go with it. But what if he thinks my songs are crap? It'll just give him more ammunition. He could do a lot of damage if he decides he still hates me – record them on his phone and play them all over the school or something.

'Maybe we can even record some of the songs Mikhal's written so we can practise at home,' Andrew says.

'You've written your own music?' asks Mr Jackson. He's so enthusiastic it almost hurts to look at him.

'Uh, yeah,' I say, only hoping I can measure up to whatever he's expecting. 'It's not very good.'

'Music is music. Every sound you make has its own perfection.' He says this so seriously that I have to believe him. I wonder how he manages to put these things into words. 'But if you can weave them together, there's no limit to what you can achieve.'

I know this, now. You can use music to bridge the gap between worlds. To save a life! Does he know this, too? Looking at him, at the fervour in his face, I almost think he might . . .

I shake my head. No. He doesn't know what we were doing that night. He doesn't know about Shar. He can't.

We set up our equipment, and I nervously tell Andrew that I'll run through the first of my songs, so he knows the melody and the tempo. Then we can work on how the drums will fit in.

'Fine,' he says shortly.

I pick up my guitar and clear my throat.

> *'I'm losing sight*
> *Of what's real*
> *In the blinding lights of this city . . .'*

I finish, and put the guitar down. Andrew isn't saying anything. Mr Jackson looks completely stunned, and I clear my throat. 'It needs work, but I think –'

'It's very good,' Mr Jackson says. His eyes are fixed, unblinking, on my face, as if searching for something. 'Where did you find your inspiration, Mikhal?'

I shift uncomfortably. It's a song I reworked yesterday. It's about the City in the sky, of course. Shar, but he can't know that.

Warning sirens are going off in my brain. *He knows. Somehow, he knows about Shar.* But how? And how much does he know?

I give him the same answer I gave Sharna. A true answer, if not the whole truth. 'I write about things that make me feel.'

He nods, slowly. Andrew is looking between us. He knows something's going on, but he can't figure out exactly what it is. 'Well, I reckon we could use a fast beat for that one, right?'

Jerked back to reality, I nod and try to concentrate on the song.

Mr Jackson helps us. His suggestions are invaluable. He knows exactly how this song should sound, and shows us some tricks with the sound equipment to wring everything we can out of our instruments. He even joins in on the bass guitar, and it sounds, as he said earlier, perfect.

It's a great session, but when Anna arrives to pick me up I'm feeling more confused than ever. I've left my phone in my bag, and there's a message from Keira: '*Meet us at Mrs Henders*'.

Chapter Fourteen:
Mr Jackson

I CALL Mum and ask if I can go to see Jake and Daniel. Anna drops me out the front.

'Is something wrong?' she asks me as she pulls up to the curb.

I realise I'm peering intently at the park. Of course, there's nothing unusual, except for the birds, but I'm almost used to seeing them by now, and they're so silent it's easier to ignore them.

'Just thinking about Saturday,' I say.

'Oh, yes. Your big performance,' she says. 'I'm looking forward to it. So is Lily.'

I feel sick as I make my way past the plastic flamingos to the front door. 'It's changed,' Keira says when I walk in. The others – minus Sharna – are all gathered in the lounge room, taking turns with the telescope again. 'It's more like . . . like a hedge.'

I take a look. Where the branches touch the ground, more branches have sprung up; it spreads out along the bicycle path and it's heading for the pine plantation.

Cari has been completely silent since I arrived, but now she speaks up. 'Or a wall.'

'What?' Jake whirls around, lowering the telescope from his eye. 'What do you mean?'

Cari looks stricken. Her beautiful pale face is even more pale. 'Oh, Jake,' she says. 'I think I've done this.'

'No, of course not, Cari. How could you be responsible?'

'Yes.' She holds up a hand to stop our protestations and questions. 'Is it possible? I think it is. I told you the Guardians planned to build a wall. It would separate the City from your world. This was their plan – this was how they were going to cut us off from the *vinarhi*.'

'How could they have planned this, though?' Jake is bewildered. So am I.

'They knew we would try to rescue Cari,' Aaron puts in, his voice grave. 'They knew we would do everything we could. It's possible they sent the seed crystal into the Ether. When we bought Cari through, we allowed the crystal to come through too. And take root.'

Cari's voice is anguished. 'This is my fault. I've brought disaster to your world – again.'

'Don't say that!' I interject. 'You couldn't possibly have known. Neither could *we*. And if these Guardians are a ruthless as you say, they'd have found another way if this one hadn't worked.'

'Can't we cut it down?' Daniel speaks up. 'It's just a tree, right?'

'It's a tree we can't see without the telescope,' Jake reminds him. 'Come on.'

We all walk across the road to the park, through the fluttering avenue of birds. They watch us as we cross to the pagoda and stare at the area where the wall should be. But though the patch of burned earth is there, nothing else is. We walk around with our arms outstretched. It's just as well the park is empty of everyone except those silent, watchful birds. We look like weirdos, but it confirms our worst fears.

This wall, the thing that's going to cut us off from the *vinarhi*, and ruin the balance between the worlds, and eventually destroy it, is completely intangible.

'How are we going to stop it?' I ask.

'Maybe we can't,' Aaron says. He looks despondent.

'You're correct.'

This voice is new, deep, calm and familiar. I turn to find its owner standing just behind us. Mr Jackson. How did he get there? How did he approach us so silently?

He has been following us. My instincts were right. I should have listened to them.

'You were watching us on Friday night, weren't you?' I say. I can barely contain the anger rising inside me.

He looks regretful. But he looks taller, stronger, standing there in the night in his long black coat, his hand in his pockets. He looks bigger and far more menacing than my music teacher ever looked. His eyes are shadowed.

I realise why: he's not my music teacher. Not anymore. Not now.

'I'm afraid it was necessary,' Mr Jackson says. There is a stoniness in his voice that I haven't heard before. No flowery descriptions now; no analysing the air and the earth and the feelings and emotions that can be conjured through words and music. Just cold facts stated in a stern voice. 'When I learned what you were doing, I had to use the opportunity. I had no choice.'

I take a step forwards, crossing my arms over my chest. Anger surges through me. 'It *was* you, watching us the other night.'

'At first I wasn't sure. When I suspected you had broken into the music wing – I was too late to catch you. My . . . my *fithdri* . . . my connection to the Ether is so unreliable in this world. It is hard to work the Ether here – like fighting against gravity. I have to use other methods. By the time I arrived here the other night, I only saw you, Aaron, and your friend, the girl, walking back from the pagoda. Perhaps I wanted to believe this was all you were doing.' He gives a small, sad smile. 'I didn't want you to be involved any more deeply than that.'

Keira moves to stand next to me, looking at him defiantly.

'You're Sharian, aren't you?' She hurls these words accusingly in his face. 'Aren't you? You're a Guardian. You're helping them!'

He shakes his head. 'Once, this was true. I was a Guardian. I worked closely with the Arbitrator. I was worthy of great respect. But that changed when a certain prisoner was allowed to escape – a woman who had broken the Edict and made a foul device. I was blamed, and tried, and I was exiled to this world.'

'Oh, so, what?' Keira continues angrily. 'This is about revenge? You're going to help them destroy us because you hate this world, too?'

The hard look on his face cracks for a moment. 'No!' He says this desperately, earnestly. 'I don't despise you. This world is more than I ever could have imagined. I've found things here I didn't think were possible . . .'

'Music,' I supply, quietly, and he turns to me and nods.

'Music. Here, music has a freedom is does not have on Shar. I can write and perform without restriction. The sounds! Oh, the harmonies and melodies I can create in this place!' His voice is desperate, but then, all of a sudden, the hardness is back. I know this look, I remember this look from the memories Keira and Aaron gave me. It's the aloofness that all Guardians wear. 'But I have no choice. I still have to do my duty. Shar, the City, is what matters.'

'How can you say that?' It's Aaron who speaks now. 'How can you say that the people of the City deserve to live, but no one on this world does?'

'Traitor!' The cold, hard side of Mr Jackson is back. He glares at Aaron, and then at Cari. 'Siding with the humans over our people, when you know that Shar hangs in the balance. You will both be punished for your indiscretions when you face the Court.'

'I've faced it once already,' Aaron says. 'I'll face it again if I have to.'

'And I have faced it twice.' Cari says. 'I spoke for humanity at that time. I'll speak again. But not before I try with all my heart to stop this.'

He hangs his head and speaks in a low whisper. 'They have my daughter. They know I've been affected by living in this world – that my sentimentality has gotten the better of me. Here, I'm free to feel my love for her. And I can't allow them to harm her.'

'Will they really hurt her?' I ask.

'It's possible,' Aaron says, his voice dead. Something tells me he knows first-hand.

'They have a way –' Keira sounds disgusted. 'They imprison those who've broken the law. Sometimes they impose death upon them.'

I remember. Of course I remember. She showed me the old man she'd laid next to in their Infirmary. He'd been subjected to this final fate. 'They'd do that to a *child*?'

'They would.' Aaron says grimly. 'I wouldn't have believed it before – before all this occurred, but I do now. I'm certain of it.'

'Then you know that I have to guard this place. I have to do everything I can to ensure the Wall takes shape.'

'But you'll die!' Daniel says loudly. 'If the wall destroys our world, you'll die too!'

'But my daughter will be safe.' He says this resolutely. Behind him, the previously silent birds start to scream. They raise their wings in flurries. They whip the air and clack their beaks. And I realise now what Mr Jackson's other methods for receiving signals from the Ether is – he's using the birds.

Aaron dives in front of Keira as if that will protect her. Jake grabs Daniel's arm with one hand, and Cari's with the other. 'Go!' he says. 'Get inside!'

We run.

It's hard – it's like running in a dream, when someone's chasing you and the ground seems to slide under your feet. I feel like I'm getting nowhere. I can see the others up ahead, and I fix my eyes on them, trying not to see the descending black cloud.

Mrs Henders has her door open for us. She must have been watching. She pulls us inside, and slams it shut.

We sit, puffing and panting, in the hallway, among the speaker equipment, staring at the door. There are a few thuds and thumps as the birds hit the solid wood, and then ominous silence.

Mrs Henders looks grim.

'How could we not have known he was from Shar?' Keira gasps, sitting against the wall, breathing hard. 'He's been teaching at the school for ages!'

'He's been here long enough to become one of you,' Mrs Henders says coolly. 'Just like I have. I knew him, when I saw him. He was at my trial on Shar. I never imagined . . .' she sighs, as if she wants to say more, but can't find the words.

'What are we going to do?' asks Cari. 'How are we going to remove the wall?'

'We didn't know how we would do it before. Now that it's being guarded, it's impossible!' Aaron says.

'So, what?' Keira fires. 'We just give up?'

'We can't give up,' Cari says softly. 'You must use the music that you used to bring me here.'

'We built a bridge with the music,' I point out. 'How can we use it to cut down the Wall?'

'What can create can also destroy.' Cari's voice is low and urgent. 'The Guardians know this. That is why they regulate artistic pursuits so zealously. It is why the Guardians fear music so intensely.'

Of course. It makes perfect sense. Mr Jackson knows it, too. He knows we used music to break through the barrier and bring Cari back.

'Mr Jackson knows we'll go back to the park,' I say. 'He'll be ready for us.'

'We could call the police,' Daniel suggests.

Jake shakes his head. 'What would we tell them? Our music teacher is trying to stop us from destroying a wall of invisible trees that reach through to another dimension?'

I can't help it. A laugh bubbles out of me, and Keira joins in. Cari smiles and even Aaron's lips twitch. But all of a sudden I stop.

I've never thought the expression 'a bolt from the blue' had much meaning, but that's what it is – it strikes me, full-on, in the chest.

'There's still the concert,' I say. 'There's going to be hundreds of people there on Saturday. He can't interfere with the concert – he's got no authority there – and besides, there's going to be security. My Mum's been arranging it with a local security company all week. If we do it then, we'll be protected.'

It's brilliant. I know it is, and so do they. I can't help but feel pretty darn pleased with myself.

'The only problem is,' Mrs Henders informs us from the door of the lounge room, 'he obviously knows about the concert, too. He'll do everything he can to prevent you from destroying the wall.'

Uneasiness cuts through my elation. 'We have to try, though.'

Everyone agrees.

***

Sharna isn't in school the next day, either.

I keep trying to call her. Her phone is turned off. She won't answer Keira or Jake, either. In some ways, I'm glad. Mr Jackson doesn't seem to know about her involvement. That means she's safe, because Mr Jackson can't reveal himself in public. Even though I know this, keep reminding myself of it, it feels strange when I head up to the music wing for our after school detention-practice.

Andrew is waiting for me. 'Can't wait to get back into it,' he says excitedly, but my eyes drift over his shoulder. Mr Jackson is sitting in his office, watching us through the door across the hall as we head into the music room. He doesn't say anything. Neither do I.

But I can feel him watching me.

I'm careful to work on the less important songs with Andrew, the ones that don't resonate so closely with Shar. I have to make sure Mr Jackson doesn't catch on to our plan, doesn't know what we're going to do at the concert. That he thinks we've done all we can by bringing Cari through. I can't help thinking, though, that maybe he can use the Ether to read my mind.

It's hard. Before, I was picking notes and chords to *build* the connections that we needed to reach Cari. Now I have to figure out a way of using music to *unmake*. How can you create something to destroy? It seems fundamentally wrong. I wonder if Einstein felt this way about building the atom bomb.

Andrew is good, though. He picks up the songs quickly and he's great at picking sympathetic rhythms. He seems to know what we need, and he has good ideas when it comes to using offsetting harmonies.

'Damn, we sound *good*,' he says, amazed, after we play back some of the stuff we've recorded.

I have to agree.

We're still awkward around each other, but the hostility is gone, and I'm glad to have my friend back.

'Some of these songs really need an electric guitar, though.'

'I know.' I do know what he means. 'I wrote most of them with that in mind. I've got an electric guitar at home.'

'Really? You should bring it in.'

'Nah,' I say. 'I'm not really . . .'

He stares at me. 'What?'

I don't know how to explain to him about Roger. I don't know that there *is* an explanation. 'I just don't feel ready to use it yet.'

He looks confused, but he shrugs and says nothing more about it while I use my favourite school acoustic guitar.

ON TUESDAY night Mum plonks a stack of flyers down on the coffee table in front of me. I've got my feet up, my maths book on my lap, and I'm trying not to listen to the news, which is telling me about a truck overturning on the highway and bursting into flames. The driver got away with burns – but only just. A flock of birds dive-bombed his windscreen.

'Look!' she says happily.

I look at the flyers. They're colourful and bright. The Bridge Foundation logo – my logo – blazes proudly across the top. And then there's my name, and Andrew's, in bold black print.

It looks professional. It looks great.

'These are all over Cassidy Heights,' she says. 'We've already sold eighty-four tickets.'

My mouth goes dry. This is real. People are actually paying to see me and Andrew play.

It's crazy.

My maths book slips out of my lap, and Mum picks it up, looking at it like it means something.

'I'm so proud of you,' Mum says. 'You know that, right?'

Looking at her smiling like that, I think I do.

***

Sharna isn't at school on Wednesday, either.

There are more and more reports of animals invading houses and yards. The news is full of stories of platypuses swimming in the river on the other side of town, and snakes in people's backyards. Knowing the cause of it, our group is more concerned than anyone else when some people are admitted to hospital with bites and scratches.

'Do you think they tried to walk through the park?' Keira says.

'Maybe. Maybe they just stepped on a snake or an ant nest when they were hanging out the washing.' But I think that maybe Mr Jackson doesn't have full control over all the animals. He's called them here, but his hold might be tentative. He said himself that he can't fully rely on them for warnings and signals.

We see him drive to the park every day after school. Jake, Daniel and Aaron walk home together from the bus stop after school – they, of course, have an excuse to be seen walking in and out of their house and Mrs Henders' place. But the rest of us are careful to take back roads on our way to Mrs Henders, and we climb over her back fence to sneak through her house and watch the growing wall through the telescope.

By Friday, it's huge. It towers above us, above Cassidy Heights, shooting straight up into the clouds. We lose sight of it over the hills as it stretches towards the highway, and our view is blocked to the other side by houses.

It seems impossible that people aren't aware of it. Of course, I know it's not a real wall, and that it only exists between our world and the Ether, which most people aren't aware of anyway. But they're starting to feel the effects.

We hear reports of increased traffic accidents along the highway. There are reports of failing crops on the edge of town. Fires break out in a shopping centre — a few people are injured, and two are killed.

Cari sits in front of Mrs Henders TV, her face white as the newsreader finishes his report. 'This is the start of the imbalance,' she says. 'The shifting of boundaries. Your world is being cut off from the Ether.'

I shiver.

She turns to look at each of us. 'What if we're too late?'

I refuse to think this. We can't be too late. This has to work.

I call Sharna.

She doesn't answer.

I think about going to her house, but somehow, it doesn't seem right to intrude on that space when she's so clearly not wanting to talk to me.

And, yes, I'm scared of her dad. It hurts a little bit to think about this, but I tell myself I can't do anything just yet. After the concert, I'll figure it out. Though I have no idea how.

***

Saturday finally arrives – the day we've been waiting for.

Mum goes crazy. She's a whirlwind of activity. Keira, of course, is running around with her, making calls to the stall-owners and security company and transport organisations. We barely have time to say two words to each other.

I can't look too eager, so I wait – it's agonising, sitting in my room, trying to practise and biting my fingernails instead, but I wait – until two o'clock before I ask Anna to drive me to Mrs Henders' place.

'I'll be back here later for the concert,' she says. 'Lily is ecstatic.'

Phoenix Park is still full of birds. But they are quiet and calm. People are moving around the pagoda, setting up stands and stalls, laying down tarpaulins. Trucks and cars flatten the grass right where I know the Wall runs. But there's no sign of Mr Jackson.

Aaron helps me carry the audio set-up across the road.

We're nervous, setting it up in the pagoda. I keep looking at the trees and the birds that are in them, but they don't make a move. Soon, everything is in place, and we check the time – it's four thirty.

We go to the Miles's place for dinner – Mrs Henders is not coming to the concert ('I've had more than enough of your loud music,' she said. Then as if embarrassed to be saying something so sentimental: 'But I wish you well. With the concert and with your task.') and Nina cooks us lemon chicken and rice – and stir fry for Aaron and for Cari, who don't eat meat. She knows Cari as Rebecca, of course, since she stayed overnight with the Miles's during the snowstorm. She likes her, I can tell, though I don't know what Jake told her about where she's from and why she vanished for a few weeks.

And when I see Cari with Jake – their easy friendliness, their obvious devotion to each other is in every look and movement. Cari sits in the lounge room and watches DVDs with Daniel. She talks easily with Nina and Mr Miles, and helps set places at the table for dinner. She might not belong in this world, but her delight with the way things work here is obvious.

She talks to me while we're piling the dishes up on the sink. 'You are brown with anxiety,' she says in a low voice. 'I can feel how nervous you are. But I know you can do this.'

I smile at her. 'Thanks,' I say. But inside I'm still tangled up. I'm so scared.

I miss Sharna, and I just hope she's okay.

***

I join Cari and Daniel for a few episodes of Neon Genesis, and I actually manage to zone out for a while, because I'm startled when Nina pokes her head in.

'It's time!'

I look at my watch – six o'clock. The magician is going to be on at any moment.

We cross the park as a group. We might be any group of friends going out on a Saturday night, I realise. Except that not one of us feels like a normal teenager tonight. Normal teenagers don't have to do what we're about to do.

The park is lit up with flickering and colourful lights. Music plays from some of the sideshows, where little kids are winning cuddly toys by shooting clowns in the mouths, and adults are happily taking their parent's money. There's a huge line at the hotdog stand – Cari and Aaron both crinkle their noses as we walk past – and everyone else is milling in the main area, before the pagoda, where the magician is setting up for their act.

We look at the birds.

They're still there, watching.

'Can you see Mr Jackson?' I ask. There are hundreds of people here. Where did they all come from? This is going to be great for the

Bridge Foundation. But there's no sign of Mr Jackson.

'Miky!' It's Mum. Dad trails behind her, looking more than a little bewildered in a casual shirt and brown slacks. This isn't his scene and I have to appreciate that he made the effort to come, even if it was probably mostly because Mum wouldn't let him stay home and file paperwork. 'Doesn't it look amazing? Keira, you did a wonderful job of organising this. I couldn't have done it without you.'

Keira looks genuinely happy. 'It was fun! Now we just have to count the proceeds, right?'

Mum gives my arm a squeeze, and then I hear a high-pitched squeal and two little arms wrap themselves around my legs.

It's Lily. Anna comes after her, panting a little. 'Lily!' she says. 'Sorry, Mikhal. She's so excited that you're playing. She's been telling everyone she knows you.'

I grin down at the little girl. It's a while since I've seen her, and she's grown. Her hair is golden and curly, but she looks pale – much thinner than a child her age should be. She's wearing a plain white dress which offsets her light blue eyes.

'Hey, Lily! I've saved a seat for you right up the front.'

She grins happily, then Anna leads her away to buy some fairy floss.

***

The magician's act is great. I watch with fascination as he puts coins through solid glass, pulls rabbits out of the air, and manages to produce a woman's missing wedding ring from his pocket.

But I can't concentrate on anything.

The telescope is in my pocket, and it seems to vibrate.

I keep looking at the place at the base of the steps to the pagoda, where the Wall had sprouted from. Of course, there's nothing to be seen.

And then, all too soon, we're up.

Chapter Sixteen:
Building Bridges

ANDREW meets me at the bottom of the steps. 'Are you ready for this?' he says.

I grin lopsidedly. 'Nope.'

'Hah!' he laughs. 'Me neither.'

We climb the steps and look down at the crowd. Has it grown? It looks like every person in Cassidy Heights is here. There are video cameras trained on us, and at the back, two professional TV crews from the local TV stations. The glare of camera flashes is blinding.

We don't say anything to one another as we set up. I carefully pick up my guitar – my old faithful acoustic, and plug it in. I give it a few test strums. The sound is pleasing and familiar.

This is right. I know what I'm doing with a guitar in my hands. I can do this.

The crowd falls silent.

I freeze for a second, then turn to Andrew. 'Um, on three?'

He looks just as freaked as I do. But he raises his drumsticks and taps them – one, two, three – and that's it, because that's when the music starts, and I couldn't stop it if I wanted to. I start to play.

It's a strong song, but it's not one of the ones I reworked using Sharna's frequency magic. It's just a platform song, one to build the foundation of our weapon.

I can see Keira weaving her crystal through her hands, and I shut my eyes, concentrating on feeling the song out by touch, singing the lyrics as best I can. I miss a few words, mix up a few others, but it doesn't seem to matter – no one notices.

All too quickly, it's over.

I breathe a huge sigh and open my eyes.

The crowd is on its feet. Only then do I realise that the roaring sound isn't in my ears – it is them, clapping and cheering.

It sounds like the waters of the *vinarhi,* but less threatening, more welcoming.

Wow. I did this. I *made* this.

I look over my shoulder at Andrew. He looks stunned. I guess I look the same as I make my way to the side of the pagoda.

I slip the strap of my acoustic guitar free from my shoulder. I put it down and take a deep breath. Roger is there, gleaming green, the little smiley face grinning up at me. My hands are shaking a bit as I pick him up and return to centre stage.

'That's your awesome guitar?' I can barely hear Andrew's voice – he sounds a little dubious, just like I knew he would, but I ignore him. I know that this is what I bought Roger for.

'Okay,' I say into the microphone. 'This next one is called *For You.*'

> *'I never meant*
> *To love you*
> *But it's like fate'*

Roger seems to sing along with me.

His sound is everything I'd known it would be – strong and powerful, subtle, pliable, brilliant. He's perfect. My fingers dance over his strings, pulling the music from them. It's as if Roger knows what I need from him, and gives it to me – but it's not him, not entirely. He's an instrument. It's me.

I'm the one who's making this.

I stop thinking about the crowd. About the wall and Cari and the Ether and Mr Jackson.

I'm lost in the melody.

And that's when I see Sharna.

She's wearing a dress. It's blue and white. It's the same dress she wore to my birthday party all those weeks ago – maybe it's the only one she has. She's not really the type to have a wardrobe full of girly clothes.

Her eyes are full of tears, and I know she knows this is her song. This is the one she should have read, not the other one.

And I'm so glad that now she knows it.

She does know it, she really does, because

she's standing now – everyone is standing – and she's dancing. Her movements are small and restrained; it's not like she's got much room, with everyone crammed in around her – but she's swaying, slight, delicate movements that mean she can feel the music deep inside her.

I keep playing.

It's there. I know it is. What we've woven is not a golden thread at all. It's a wide, shimmering green carpet. It goes right down deep into the earth, down to where the insects that shouldn't be awake and moving at this time of year are scurrying around, confused and scared by the changes in the balance of the world, and further, much further to where there's nothing alive at all, just pulsing heat and spurting gas and thick, solid earth.

It's strong. It's as strong as our planet, which has borne so much change and weight and pain. It's as strong as the will of every person and every living thing it supports and gives life to, every person and every living thing that wants to live and thrive and be happy.

This is our defence against the Guardians.

But as the song comes to an end, and I look up to smile at Sharna, I see someone else standing at her side.

It's Mr Jackson. And he's staring straight at me.

***

He knows what I'm doing, now. And I know he's going to do everything to stop me. I suddenly think this was a terrible mistake, doing this tonight. All these people gathered here – they're all in danger because of me! Mum and Dad, Anna, Lily . . .

And then I think about the wall. They're all in danger anyway, and it's the Guardians doing, not mine.

I look up at the birds gathered in the trees.

Then I look over my shoulder at Andrew.

'Impressive!' he grins at me, and nods towards Roger, who, obviously, has proven himself worthy in Andrew's estimation. 'Next one?'

'No,' I say. 'We need to do *Building Bridges.*'

His eyes widen. This wasn't the way we planned it. This was supposed to be the last song, but it's too late for that now. Mr Jackson could make a move to stop us at any time.

The next song is the one that matters.

It starts slowly. Keira is out there, plucking up those strong, strident notes with the crystal and threading them together, winding them to fit the base we've created, but I can't concentrate on her. I have to get this right.

The crowd reacts to the change in tone and tempo. They're still standing, some people are dancing, but they're looking, too – looking at one another, looking at us, looking at the darkness of the park beyond the lights.

The birds stir and shift in the shadows.

Mr Jackson is moving.

He's pushing through the crowd, but they push back against him – he's fighting a rip tide of people who don't quite know why they don't want to move for him. I can see the anger, and the fear, in his eyes.

He's shouting something. But the noise of the song blasting out of the speakers drowns him out. I keep playing.

The next notes build towards the chorus, which I've written in A minor. I'm singing the words without thinking – I can't even remember what they are.

'Across the space of the universe,
I found you, impossible as it seemed
I didn't know how perfect it could be
Not to want anything else at all –'

The frequency of the notes are deliberately displeasing, this time. It sets everyone on edge. It jars my ears. It doesn't matter, though, because it's working.

All at once, I can see it's working.

And so can everyone else.

The wall, the horrifyingly beautiful delicate thing, is visible now – to everyone. The crowd turns their heads towards it, muttering and gasping in shock.

'What is that?'

'How on earth –'

They think it's part of the show.

I can't stop playing. I can't hear Andrew's drums. I think he's stopped, too amazed and confused to find his place. I'm on my own, now, I realise.

But I can do this. If I can make Sharna dance, I can do this!

The notes clash and clang. The wall shivers. Its roots and branches seek the harmony of the Ether. That's what feeds it, what keeps it alive. I'm ruining it, tearing it apart. It doesn't like what I'm doing, but it can't stop me.

But Mr Jackson can. He raises his arms.

And the birds come.

THEY descend in a huge black cloud, cawing and shrieking and dropping like stones on the crowd below. People scream, grab their loved ones, duck and yell and wave their arms and run. I search the chaos for my friends, but I can't see anything but black, flapping wings.

I keep playing. I keep sending out those horrible discordant notes. I keep doing it, even though it's awful. Roger does everything I ask. The Wall is cracking apart. A splintered branch falls, scattering the cloud of birds; for a moment I can see clearly. People are running for their cars. Some have ducked into the tents and stalls, cowering low and covering their heads.

Where are Jake and Daniel? Keira and Aaron and Andrew? Where's Sharna?

'What are you doing?'

It's Mr Jackson. He's right in front of me, and I don't know how he got there. His fists are clenched.

'You can't do this,' he says. There is anguish in his voice. 'They're going to kill my daughter!

Please don't do this!'

'No,' I yell. I have to yell to be heard. 'You did everything they asked of you, didn't you? You did everything you could to make sure the Wall took root and grew. They can't dispute that.'

Another section of the Wall crashes down, shatters, and vanishes.

We can see the rushing waters of the *vinarhi* beyond. Trailing wisps of white light.

I can see the remnants of the crowd now. There's hardly anyone left in the seats. I can see one small shape step forwards. She's not afraid of the birds. She reaches up her hands to touch them, and amazingly, they fall silent around her, flapping gently to land on the ground at her feet.

Lily.

All across the park, the birds are settling, quietening. Like a tidal wave, the effect spreads out until the birds are still, their only movement the occasional flutter of wings.

Mr Jackson sees her, and I can see it on his face – this small, pale girl might well be his daughter. Fragile and innocent and with so many possibilities ahead of her. She might be from a different world, but she's no different to the little girl he had to leave behind.

'They can do what they like. They always have.'

'No,' a calm voice says from behind him. It's Cari. 'Things are changing. Tonight, things have *been changed.*'

Jake comes up behind her, and Daniel too. Aaron, his shoulders squared, stands beside me.

'It's true. The Guardians will know, now, that there are people on this world who are willing to defend it. Not just willing, but able. And the Etherologists on Shar will have heard the music here tonight and will have seen what has happened. They won't be able to keep this entirely silent. There have always been rumours and whisperings – now they will get stronger. Too strong to ignore.'

I've lowered Roger to one side, holding him by the strap.

Mr Jackson's shoulders slump. 'You've destroyed me.'

'You can go back,' Cari says. 'If you choose, you can go back.'

He looks at her, and then up at the sky.

The wisps of light shining through the Wall wind around one another, bind together, reach out – it's a bridge.

It reaches up into the sky. Right up to the City, which we can all see clearly now. The beautiful towers beckon.

Mr Jackson's face fills with joy and longing. 'Oh,' he says. His clenched fists loosen at his sides. The birds are quiet – no, not just quiet, they're gone. It's only us and the bridge.

'This is your chance,' I say.

'I've been away for too long.' He says this with deep utter regret. But not, I notice, despair. 'I don't belong there anymore.'

'I'm sorry,' I say, and I mean it.

'I have bound myself to your world. I can't go back now, or ever.'

'But you can still touch Shar,' I tell him. 'Music can cross the boundary. All art can. Perhaps you can even talk to your daughter, if you work out which notes to use. Sharna and I can help you!'

I look to Sharna, who is gazing, rapt, at the shimmering length of the bridge. She's smiling as if it's the most wonderful thing she's ever seen.

'Sharna?' I say. She doesn't seem to hear me.

Keira has stood silent until now, and I turn to see her clutching Aaron's hand tightly. He is looking to the bridge with the same entranced expression Sharna wears. I know it's calling to him.

'I have to go back,' he says softly. 'It's where I belong.'

'No!' Keira says, her voice shaking.

'You know it as well as I do, Keira,' he says softly, squeezing her hand. 'Someone needs to make sure this doesn't happen again. Cari said it best – everything has changed now. I want to make sure everyone knows it. This is why I was sent here, Keira! This is my path. I'm only sorry that I can't take you with me.'

He reaches into his pocket, and pulls out a bit of folded paper – the paper I gave him, with the names of his relatives on it.

'Can you find these people?' he asks. 'Can you let them know that my father – Frederick

Mason – lived a good life, and he found my mother, who loved him very much?'

Keira takes it, and hugs him so tightly I don't think she'll ever let him go.

I can't watch.

I turn to Jake – he's standing on the steps with Cari.

Cari's eyes are luminous. 'When I left Shar, I caused an imbalance. I almost destroyed your world. I can't take that risk again.'

'But if the balance has been restored,' Sharna says, 'You can stay.'

Her voice is firm and strong, but her eyes – her eyes are distant, fixed on the bridge and where it leads.

'What do you mean?' I grasp her arm. But I think I already know.

Everything inside me is screaming. *No, no, no . . .*

Sharna turns to me. She is burning with that energy and verve that makes her light up inside. 'I want to go.'

'You can't.' I say this, but I know she can. I already know she's going to.

'I'm sorry, Mikhal.' She leans forwards and kisses me, quickly, gently. 'But this is what I was meant to do. This is why I was drawn by the Ether, right? This is how I'm supposed to make a difference.'

She's right. Of course she's right. It's tearing me apart that she's right.

'I don't want you to go.'

'Keep the telescope. If you look up at the sky, you'll see where I am. And when you play your guitar, you can reach me with a thread.' She smiles sadly. 'Write me another song. Please?'

I close my eyes and kiss her. She kisses me back, but it's so soft, so gentle I can barely feel it.

It's like she's already gone.

***

I watch her leave. Aaron takes her arm, and they walk away.

Keira is clutching my arm tightly. I think she's using my sleeve as a tissue, but right then I can't care. I watch them as they walk along that slender, impossible bridge; but even now, it's fading from view. I could take out the telescope, but I find I don't want to.

I turn away at last. I see Jake and Cari embracing tightly. I see Mr Jackson looking sad and alone. I see the ruined stalls, the over-turned chairs, the shredded tarpaulins, and cars with smashed windscreens. And there's Andrew, still sitting behind his drum set, mouth wide.

'What just happened?' he breathes.

I take a deep breath. 'Andrew, I think there's a lot I'm going to need to explain.'

'Miky?'

My mum, of course. She shrieks as she runs across the park, her high-heeled shoes sticking in the mud until she loses them completely. She barrels up the steps and pulls me into the tightest hug I've ever had.

'Oh, Miky, I'm so glad you're all right!'

I laugh. 'Yeah, Mum, I'm fine. Some concert, hey?'

She laughs through her sobbing. 'It doesn't matter. None of it matters. I don't care how well you do in school. It doesn't matter if you fail. Just as long as you're safe.'

I shake my head. 'Yes, it does. I don't want to fail, Mum. I know that, now.'

'You were so . . . good, Miky. Your playing, your singing. I didn't realise how good you were with music.'

I can't tell her how happy it makes me to hear that. How relieved. 'I'm sorry the concert was ruined, though.'

She looks slightly bewildered. 'I don't know what got into those birds.'

I stare at her for a moment. Did she really not see the bridge? Didn't she remember the Wall? But it's clear, from the way she's looking at me, that she doesn't.

Apparently, no one else did, either. Andrew looks at me weirdly when I start to talk about the bridge. 'What are you talking about?' he says. 'There was no bridge. I was right here.'

I shake my head, trying to think of how to make him believe it, but in the end I close my mouth. It's easier just to let him believe the birds went crazy and tore up the park. Maybe one day I'll explain it to him, but right now, I'm too tired.

'You're a freaking weirdo, you know,' Andrew laughs, slinging an arm around my shoulders. 'But you're my mate, so I'll forgive you.'

The police are there seconds later, and ambulances. There have been a few cars wrecked, and several people badly injured. We have to give our names and brief statements, but they let us go fairly quickly, more concerned with cleaning up the mess than anything else.

We find Anna on the footpath, hugging Lily tightly and scolding her for wandering off.

If only I could have told her that by doing so, Lily had saved our world.

But I don't.

Nina and Mr Miles are making their way home with Jake and Daniel – Nina, thank goodness, looks fine – and they refuse to let Mum and Dad, or Anna drive in this crowd.

'They've cordoned off the street. You won't even get through. Come in for a coffee, then you can go when things have quietened down.'

Jake speaks up. 'I'd like to go and make sure Mrs Henders is okay,' he says.

'That's thoughtful. Good on you,' Mr Miles says. 'Go on.'

I give Roger to Lily to take inside and play with, and I stand with Daniel, Keira, Jake and Cari on the footpath until they're inside. Keira is calling her mum to let her know she's fine.

'No, Mum, I'm okay, I promise,' she says

helplessly. Her mum must be worried because of Keira's earlier accident. 'I'm fine.'

But she doesn't exactly sound fine.

I know, because I don't think I'll ever be fine again, either.

'Keira,' I say, after she's hung up. 'Where's your crystal?'

Keira smiles sadly and reaches into her pocket. She pulls out a few small hard lumps of something like charcoal. 'I think it's dead.'

And then she starts to cry. And I do, a little bit, too.

***

Mrs Henders has seen the whole thing through her front window. She looks at us sternly as we troop inside.

'You played a dangerous game tonight,' she says. 'You're lucky you won.'

'It might not be the end of it, though,' Jake muses. 'There are still Bridges out there. And now we know that more can be made. There might be more repercussions we don't even know about yet.'

'Yeah, but we've proved we can face them, haven't we?' Daniel says, ever the optimist.

'No one in the crowd seems to realise what we did tonight.' I say this quietly, but everyone hears me. 'How is that possible?'

Mrs Henders shakes her head. 'Humans are

unfortunately blind to those things they don't want to see, or want to understand. But you have seen, and you have understood. It's your responsibility now, to make those things known to others.'

'How do we do that?' asks Daniel thoughtfully. But no one replies, because we all know we've got to come up with our own answer to that.

Through the silence, I can hear the unmusical sounds of Lily playing my guitar next door.

And I think I know exactly how I can do it.

***

'That's wrong,' says Andrew. 'Totally wrong.'

We're in the studio, sitting in front of a computer, running backwards and forwards through our latest song, *The Other Side of the Line*. We've been working on it for a week, but it's still not coming together.

'Everything okay?' Mr Jackson pokes his head around the door.

'Getting there,' says Andrew, at the same time I say 'No.'

'Can I hear what you've got so far?' he asks, pulling up a chair.

Andrew hits the space bar to play the track through once more. I sit back and look at Mr Jackson. His head cocked to one side, he's listening intently to every nuance of sound.

I keep expecting him to say something, the mention what happened in the park that night, but he doesn't. Maybe it's too painful for him to talk about. Maybe he feels guilty. Maybe he's regretting that he didn't cross the bridge and go back to Shar after all.

I don't press the issue.

He seems happy enough not to talk about it, and frankly, I'm sick of reliving it too. There was lots of media attention after the concert. Andrew and I were interviewed three times, and we leaped on the chance to promote ourselves as musicians. We came up with the name *Bridging Gap*, and it's been great publicity. I've even designed us a logo. We'd been asked if we intend to start pursuing music as a career, and we, of course, said yes.

There were questions we couldn't answer quite so concisely, of course. Nina and Mr Miles were curious about Aaron's sudden disappearance, and Mrs Henders' adoption of Cari, or Rebecca. But they were more than happy to help her enrol in school, and provide clothes and other essentials through the Bridge Foundation. They were mostly too distracted with their new baby girl, which arrived yesterday, to ask too many questions.

Nina and Mum are both overjoyed at our first successful fundraiser. We managed to get close to nine thousand dollars profit, and now Keira's busy deciding what to do with it. She's allocating a thousand dollars towards Lily's special schooling.

Anna had tears in her eyes when we told her. 'I don't know if I can accept this.'

'You have to. This is only the start,' Keira said bluntly. 'When everything's up and running, we'll be able to help people all over the world. What happens if everyone starts refusing our help?'

Even less easy to answer were the questions about Sharna.

We didn't lie to the police. We told them that the last time we saw her was at the pagoda after the disaster at the concert. Her dad stuck up missing posters and there have been articles in the newspaper and on Crimestoppers. Every time I see the photos of her, my heart clenches up a little, and I hope she's doing what she wants to do.

I'm pretty darn sure she is.

'The problem is here,' Mr Jackson says, bringing me back to the present with a jolt. 'Where you switch between keys. You need to make it smoother – tie it together.'

He's right, of course. He really does know what he's talking about when it comes to music. It speaks to him the same way it does to me.

We both have a vetted interest in making it work for us now – music, melody, harmony. It's a link to people we both care about, and it's the only one we've got. It's a link between us, too.

***

We finish our session and Andrew heads to the car park, where his mum is waiting. She waves to me through the windscreen, and I give her a wave back as I make our way to the front gate of the school. The last of the buses have left and the schoolyards are empty – truly empty, without hordes of birds glaring down at us from the trees and rooftops. The sun is shining and the air carries a bit of warmth. Spring is coming.

Jake is there, leaning against the gate. His head is bent and he's talking to Cari, who's wearing jeans and a roll-neck jumper, laughing and looking like a regular girl at our school.

'Hey, Mikhal,' Jake says.

'Is Daniel coming?' I ask him. We're all heading out to get pizza and talk about the Bridge Foundation. We need to come up with more money if it's going to keep helping people.

'Yeah, he's meeting us there. He went to the mall with some girl,' Jake says, rolling his eyes. 'He's too young for that.'

Keira comes pounding up behind me, snaking an arm around my neck and pulling me into a headlock. I shake her off. 'Careful of Roger!' I tell her, adjusting my guitar case.

She grins at me. 'So,' she says. Despite her light tone I can see the seriousness in her eyes. 'You're writing more music?'

I nod. I know what she's asking, why she's asking it. She wants to know about Aaron – Archon. I've tried to reach Sharna a couple of times by playing Roger, alone in my room, late at night when everything is quiet. I want to tell her about how I finished my essay, the one about something that means something to me. How I got a B+, which I think was just for handing something in, but it made my mum and dad happy. I've written a couple of songs, but none of them have worked. I wonder if it's because of the disruption in the Ether, or the disruption in *me*.

I don't really know why I'm trying. I just want to know she's okay. At first I had these ideas about how I could maybe build a permanent bridge between our worlds, but the more I speak to Cari, the more I think that would only cause more problems. Our world is still kind of screwed up – we're still trashing the environment, changing the climate, and letting people starve and die of disease in third world countries. It's probably best we fix those problems before we start making contact with Shar again.

Keira is still looking at me, so I give my head a little shake. She presses her lips together, but in the next moment she links her arm with mine, pulling me along. 'Come on. I need pizza.'

'Have you done any more research into finding Frederick Mason's relatives?' Jake asks me.

I nod. 'I called Emma Lovell yesterday. She was his niece, and she's our age now. She lives about an hour away and she wants to meet up next week.'

Keira punches my arm. 'Hey, maybe she's hot!'

I roll my eyes in exasperation. 'I'm not looking for a girlfriend right now,' I say.

Her expression is sympathetic. I know she's hurting more on the inside than she lets on. The best thing we can do right now is help each other out.

Because, really, we're just a group of friends who maybe saved the world a few times.

Thank you for reading
THE WALL BETWEEN THE WORLDS.
We hope you enjoyed it.

If you would like to be kept informed of further releases by Ruth Fox, or other new books from Hague Publishing, why not subscribe to our newsletter at:
www.HaguePublishing.com/subscribe

And if you loved the book and have a moment to spare we would really appreciate a short review. Your help in spreading the word is gratefully received.

About The Author

RUTH Fox is the author of *The Bridges Trilogy* and the award-winning *Monster-boy: Lair of the Grelgoroth*.

She loves to paint, cook and play computer games (very badly). She has a Bachelor of Arts/Diploma of Arts in Professional Writing and Editing. So far she has worked at several far less meaningful or interesting jobs – but writing is her life. She loves science fiction, fantasy, romance, adventure, young adult, adult, literature, old books, new books, and everything in between.

She currently lives with her husband and three very curious and adventurous sons (who also love books) in Ballarat, Victoria.

You can visit her website at: ruth-fox.com, or on Facebook at RuthFoxAuthorandArtist.

Hague

Publishing

www.HaguePublishing.com
PO Box 451 Bassendean
Western Australia 6934